DEVIL'S DEAL

After barely surviving the Civil War, all Confederate sharp-shooter Ethan van Kirk wants is a quiet life at his homestead with his eight-year-old daughter, Lucy. Then a shadow from his past appears. Suddenly he is forced to use his deadly shooting skills again in a deal with the Devil. Ethan must kill an innocent man to save his daughter's life. And the clock is ticking . . .

Books by Lee Walker
in the Linford Western Library:

GUN LAW
PAY DIRT

LEE WALKER

DEVIL'S DEAL

Complete and Unabridged

LINFORD
Leicester

First published in Great Britain in 2013 by
Robert Hale Limited
London

First Linford Edition
published 2014
by arrangement with
Robert Hale Limited
London

A catalogue record for this book is available
from the British Library.

ISBN 978–1–4448–2214–4

Published by
F. A. Thorpe (Publishing)
Anstey, Leicestershire

Set by Words & Graphics Ltd.
Anstey, Leicestershire
Printed and bound in Great Britain by
T. J. International Ltd., Padstow, Cornwall

This book is printed on acid-free paper

For Olivia

Prologue

Chinn Ridge, Virginia, 1861

The two rebel soldiers belly-crawled through the dust to the edge of the cliff and peered down the vertical escarpment to the fast-flowing river below. Both were well versed at estimating range and it took them only a few seconds to reckon the drop.

'Sixty-two feet,' announced Corporal Ethan van Kirk.

'Agreed,' said Major Thomas Kramer.

Across from them, the boulder-strewn river-bank sloped gently upwards away from the water, but it wasn't just the terrain that was of interest to the two men. A thin wisp of blue smoke rose from a driftwood fire at the river's edge. Squatting beside it was a blue-uniformed soldier.

'Well, well . . . what've we got here?'

murmured Major Kramer.

He was only twenty-four years old but he had the assured confidence of a man ten years his senior. Although he had been an officer in the Virginian regiment for less than six months, he had the natural authority that was his birthright as the second son of one of the wealthiest landowners in the South; a position that also provided him with the means to maintain his expensive taste in uniforms, liquor and women.

He pulled off his hat and swept clawed fingers through a damp mop of shoulder-length blond hair as he glanced over his shoulder at the other three members of his unit. They had been left lazing under the shade of a large cottonwood tree while he and van Kirk reconnoitred the cliff-edge.

'Take a closer look, will you, Corporal?'

Ethan van Kirk was the same age as Kramer but that was about the only thing they had in common. He was a quiet man, the son of a pig farmer. He had a smallholding of his own where his wife, Helen, and four-year-old daughter, Lucy, waited anxiously for him to come home.

He pulled a set of field glasses from the leather pouch on his belt. Apart from their rare British Whitworth rifle and a cartridge ammunition pouch, the glasses were one of the few pieces of kit members of the newly formed sharpshooter units were allowed to carry. Even rations were deemed non-essential; food could always be scavenged on the move. The deadly effectiveness of these small squads depended on them being able to move quiet, fast and light.

Ethan raised the glasses to his eyes and swept the shoreline.

'Got 'im. Looks like a Yankee officer, sir.'

Major Kramer squinted up at the midday sun then replaced his hat.

'Lord, it sure is hot today. Lemme see that, Corporal . . . '

Ethan passed the glasses and pointed

a line for the major to follow. After a few moments, Kramer smiled broadly.

'Well, well. Looks like we got ourselves a Yankee major.'

'What's he doin' there all by hisself, sir?'

'I do believe he thinks he's on some sorta vacation. Got his coffee on the boil and a line in the river. Tryin' for some catfish for supper. Prob'ly tired of them rotten Yankee army rations already.'

'Gotta horse?'

The major shifted the glasses further up the river-bank. 'Tied up on some cottonwoods, yonder.'

'Reckon he's on his own, sir?'

Major Kramer scanned a wider area.

'No sign of his men. Still lickin' their wounds after the whuppin' we gave 'em at Manassas. They wasn't expectin' that, was they, boy?'

'No, *sir*,' said Ethan, smiling.

The young major called everyone under his command 'boy' regardless of their age. Some of the older men in the unit grumbled about it behind the major's back, but Ethan didn't take offence. Although he would never admit it to the rest of the men, he liked Kramer. He was a lot less formal than most of the other officers and Ethan had never seen him lose his temper, or ask the men do something he couldn't do himself. Every now and then, when he'd been lucky at the faro table, the major would order double whiskey and tobacco rations.

'They won't be expectin' trouble this far behind their line. Ain't even posted sentries,' Kramer was saying. He passed the field-glasses back to Ethan and wiped his forehead with a yellow neckerchief.

'What we gonna do, sir?'

'Well, it wouldn't do no harm to get this critter back to headquarters and see how much he knows.' Kramer paused. 'But we ain't gonna get to him without making one unholy racket and the longer we hang around up here, the more chance we got of gettin' caught.'

'Even if we did manage to get 'im, he'd slow us down real bad.'

'Agreed, Corporal.'

'So what'll we do, sir?'

Kramer stroked his chin thoughtfully. 'I reckon we got no choice but to kill 'im!'

Ethan stared at the major. Up until two months ago, before he had arrived at the Bull Run river, Ethan had never shot at another man let alone killed anybody. Like thousands of his countrymen, he had been swept up by the Confederate Army's recruitment drive and after a few weeks' basic training found himself heading off to battle. He had no idea of knowing what he would do when he stood on a battlefield for the first time. The old hands called it 'meeting the elephant', but whatever they called it, Ethan had never been so frightened in all his life. But he had managed to stand his ground at Manassas, firing relentlessly into the approaching ranks of the Northern Army trying to obey the officers constantly screaming above the roar of the guns to 'Aim low, aim low!' He must have hit some Yankees — maybe even killed a few — but it was hard to tell as they fell through the blue clouds of cannon and gunsmoke.

But killing in the heat of battle was one thing; what the major was asking him to do was something else again.

Ethan realized Kramer was talking to him.

'That's why you're here, boy. Ain't this why our units were put together in the first place? Have you forgot it's our job to disrupt the Yankee war machine in any way we can?'

'No, sir.'

'And that includes the assassination of senior personnel.'

Ethan gazed down at the unarmed man on the river-bank and swallowed hard.

'Don't look so long-faced, boy. You could be standin' in a field with Yankee snipers using you as practice for a turkey shoot. I got you out of that, remember?'

'Yes, sir.'

'So, let's get on with the job. We've got a clear shot. Going by the grass up yonder there's next to no wind to account for. So I reckon this is where we find out if all those hours of target practice was worth it, or if we was just wastin' lead,' he said, smiling widely, showing a row of white, tombstone teeth.

'Who's gonna do it, sir?'

Major Kramer looked over his shoulder at the rest of his unit.

'Well, I guess we got Hamill or Stokes. They're pretty good at shootin' at targets but I don't know if their nerve'd hold when it came down to it.'

He nodded in the direction of a stocky, red-haired soldier standing urinating against a tree trunk. 'Truth be told, the honour of first blood should go to Sergeant Finnegan. He's just itchin' to show you boys how it's done.

I swear to God, I never met a man who had such few qualms 'bout killin'.' Leaning on his elbow, Kramer turned to face Ethan. 'But you know what, Corporal, I think you should do it.'

'Me, sir?'

'Sure,' said Kramer, slapping him on the shoulder. 'You're the best damn shot in the regiment, boy. I've watched you. You're a natural. I don't think I've seen you miss yet.'

Ethan tried not to blush. 'Well, thank ya, but — '

'And you got nerve too, ain't ya?'

'I guess, but — '

'Well, then, what's the problem, boy? Thought you'd see it as an honour.'

'Yes, sir. I do, sir . . . but, well, training's one thing but this . . . '

'You goin' yellah on me, Soldier?'

'No, sir. It's just — '

'Spit it out, boy!'

Ethan frowned and took a deep breath.

'Well, sir. Guess it's just that I ain't ever shot at a man that wasn't shootin' back at me. It don't seem right, somehow, sneakin' up like this.'

Major Kramer smiled at him as though he was a child.

'You ever killed a sick dog?'

'A couple.'

'Well then. That's all he is. A sick, Yankee dog. You'd be doin' him a favour, putting him out of his misery.'

'I don't know, sir . . . '

Kramer's smile faded.

'I'm giving you an order, boy. You tellin' me you gonna disobey a direct order?'

Ethan stiffened. 'No, sir.'

Kramer smiled again.

'Thatta boy. Now don't you go lettin' me down. You get yourself sorted and I'll go tell the men what's happenin'. Soon as you shoot, we gotta hightail outta here. They catch us in these uniforms this far behind the lines, we'll all be wearin' hemp neckties before nightfall. Y'hear?'

'Yes, sir.'

'Well, then. Keep that in mind. Now,

you got one shot. Make it count. Ain't I got you the best rifle in the whole damn army?'

'Yes, sir,' said Ethan, tapping the Manchester-made Whitworth.

'Had to smuggle 'em through that Yankee blockade. There's only two hundred and fifty of them in the South — and you got one of the fifty fitted with 'scopes. You know they cost more than twelve hundred dollars apiece, don't you?'

'Yes, sir.' Ethan had heard this a hundred times before but he would not have dared interrupt the major. He knew the rifle was the major's further proof that his squad was marked out for special treatment and the major expected the results in return.

'Well, then. We're all dependin' on ya.'

Kramer gave Ethan one last smile then raised himself onto his hands and knees and crawled back from the edge of the bluff. When he was sure he could not be seen from the river, he stood up and made his way back to the rest of the men.

Ethan watched him go then looked down again at his target and took a deep, shuddering breath. He touched the red triangular flash on his shoulder that marked him out as a marksman and felt a familiar surge of pride. He guessed this was where he earned the privileged treatment all sharpshooters received. No parades. No drill, or guard duties, or a hundred other chores that made up the daily grind of an ordinary infantryman.

He placed the butt of the rifle into the sand and reached into the small leather pouch on his belt to load and prime. Even the ammunition was special. Each slug was made to exacting standards so that they were identical. The powder charge was measured accurately and the cartridge was made from parchment paper lubricated in paraffin wax. It was this attention to detail that made the gun so expensive — and so deadly, creating mayhem among artillery and creating a constant psychological threat among the enemy senior officers.

He reached for a small metal stand that was strapped across his back, pushed its legs into the sand and placed the stock into the cradle. Sweat was beginning to fleck his brow as he screwed on the narrow telescopic sight to the left of the barrel. Lying on his belly he peered down the black metal tube, adjusting the lens until his target was in clear focus. Ethan watched the Yankee officer prod the fire with a stick, oblivious to what was about to happen.

He looked about the same age as Ethan. Just a few months ago, before they were on opposite sides of this madness, Ethan would have probably gone down to join him and helped him catch a few fish. While they cooked on hot stones, they might have shared a pipe and swapped stories about their home and families. Maybe, like Ethan, he had kin at home, praying for his safe return.

Ethan shook his head angrily. It was no good thinking like this. He had his orders.

He reached inside his tunic and pulled out a small gold locket that hung around his neck on a chain then he kissed it gently and let it drop back down against his chest. Glancing over his shoulder, he saw the rest of the unit all looking in his direction. Kramer lifted his hand, indicating that Ethan should fire when he was ready.

He raised the rifle, steadying it with both elbows, and looked down the sight, keeping his head a little way back to avoid the black eye that most inexperienced sharpshooters got from the recoil.

The Yankee officer's head filled the 'scope and then slowly, slowly he started to apply pressure on the trigger. Sweat kept trickling from his brow and his palms were sticky as he continued to squeeze. He took a deep breath and as he exhaled, he let the hammer fall. The gun leapt like a live thing trying to escape his grip. Through a cloud of blue smoke, Ethan saw the side of the Yankee major's head bloom red for an instant and then he keeled forward, falling to his knees, and then toppled over so that his head and shoulders came to rest in the river. Dark swirls of blood oozed into the water.

Ethan scrambled to his feet and let out the rebel yell, his high, wild cry echoing through the canyon.

'I did it! I got the sonofabitch! I got 'im, Major!'

He turned to face his cheering comrades, but, as he did, his voice died in his throat.

Behind Major Kramer and his men, a dozen Yankee cavalrymen were bearing down at a full gallop. They spun round as they heard hoofbeats and knew there was nowhere to run. There was barely time to raise their rifles.

Ethan was frozen to the spot as he watched each man fire one round knowing they would have no time to reprime the muzzle-loading Whitworth.

Two of the riders toppled from their saddles into the long grass but the rest came on relentlessly, sabres flashing in the sunlight.

Ethan saw Kramer draw his pistol, take steady aim and then wait until a horse was nearly upon him before shooting the rider in the face at point-blank range. The man screamed and fell, dead before he hit the ground as his horse reared in wide-eyed panic. Then Kramer did a strange thing. Ethan stared in disbelief as he watched Kramer grab the reins and swing himself into the saddle. Without a backward glance, he sank his heels viciously into the side of the horse's flanks and left the men under his command to their fate.

As he galloped away, Ethan looked on in despair at his comrades. He heard an agonized scream and saw a Yankee officer's sword slice down on Sergeant Finnegan's face, gashing it open from his forehead to his jaw. Blood poured through his fingers as the Irishman grasped his face before slumping into the long grass.

Ethan saw Private Hamill take three bullets to his chest before he fell. Stokes bravely stood his ground a little longer before being clubbed from behind by a rifle butt. His skull cracked under the impact and loose teeth slipped from his mouth as he fell.

And then suddenly, it was quiet again and Ethan realized he was the only one left standing.

'There's another one!'

The Yankees swung their horses in his direction. Ethan's rifle slipped uselessly from his fingers as he stepped backwards. He turned to run then realized he was only a few feet away from the edge of the cliff. Unlike the other men, it seemed he would have a choice of how he would die this day: be hacked down by enemy swords or plunge to certain death into the river. The drumming hoofbeats of the approaching horses demanded that a choice be made.

Ethan took three large strides towards the edge of the cliff. Shots rang out and a bullet sang past his ear as he launched himself into thin air. For a brief instant he felt the elation of weightlessness and then he was falling like a rock, arms and legs flailing, plummeting towards the dark water below him. He instinctively shut his eyes, bracing himself for the sickening snap of bone against the rocks that surely must lurk below the river's surface.

He hit the water. The cold shock stole what little breath he had. He sank through it, then slowed, then, miraculously, felt his feet touch the shingle river-bed just as his lungs were about to burst.

He bent his knees and pushed off, hauling himself through the murky green water to the brightness of daylight overhead. His legs ached as he kicked his water-filled boots and he felt the strong current pull at his clothes as though the river did not want to let him go. After what seemed an eternity, he broke the surface, gasping for air.

Small splashes exploded around him and, looking up, he saw a line of rifles pointing in his direction. He'd never learned to swim but Ethan knew if he didn't reach the river-bank soon, he would never get out of this water alive. He thrashed his arms frantically and the current took him close enough to shore to feel solid ground. He scrambled out of the freezing water hardly daring to look at the body of the young officer he'd killed and ran up the stony bank. Intermittent shots rang out around him.

He saw the soldier's horse and headed for it. The beast trembled and whinnied and pulled against its tether but the reins held. Ethan tore them from the branch and swung into the saddle. The horse reared, but Ethan dug his hands into the horse's mane, kicked its flanks and yelled. As the horse lunged forward, Ethan felt a dull thud in his back. His lungs emptied of air and a blinding pain flashed through his brain. He let out a low moan and fell forward onto the horse's neck.

Half-conscious, Ethan managed to hold on as the horse galloped along the side of the river, neither knowing nor caring which direction the beast was headed.

★　★　★

The next time Ethan opened his eyes, it was nightfall. The horse had stopped. It stood shivering, nervously pawing the ground, foam-flecked and blowing hard. As his eyes began to focus, Ethan realized someone was holding the horse's halter. Behind him, he could see rows of white, military tents. There was a tall flagpole in the middle of the camp, but Ethan could not make out the colours of the flag.

'You OK?' the soldier asked.

'Union . . . ?' Ethan gasped.

'Confederate. We're on your side.'

'Major Kramer . . . he . . . '

'Kramer's here. Got in a few hours back. You part of his unit?'

Ethan nodded.

'He said you was all dead.'

'Maybe we are,' Ethan managed to say, before a wave of nausea swept through him. He slid from the horse before the soldier could grab him and landed heavily on the soft earth. He rolled onto his back and looked up at a large moon.

There was no pain now. He just felt sad that he would never get to see Lucy again. He smiled at the memory of his beautiful daughter. As the moon faded into darkness, he could have sworn he could hear her calling for him in the night.

1

Four years later

'*Daddy . . . ?*'

With a gasp for breath, Ethan van Kirk jerked himself from the restless doze which was the closest thing he ever got to a night's sleep.

As his eyes flickered open, it took him a few seconds to realize where he was. Above his head, insects flitted around a smoking kerosene lamp hanging from a crossbeam. Beyond the halo of pale yellow light, there was nothing but warm, black night.

'You OK, Daddy?'

Ethan realized his eight-year-old daughter was standing next to him in her cotton nightdress. Concern was etched across her face. He straightened himself in the old rocking chair and smiled reassuringly, looking round the familiar front porch of the homestead. In the darkness, a locomotive let out a mournful whistle somewhere near Cotton Junction, nearly three miles away.

'Sure, Lucy. I'm OK. How long you been standin' there?'

'Not long. You were callin' out for me.'

'Was I?'

'Bad dreams again?'

Ethan rubbed his aching eyes and realized he had been gripping the arms of the rocking chair as hard as he had once clenched the stock of his Whitworth rifle. He felt the familiar spasm in his shoulder where the Yankee bullet had ripped through his muscles and ligaments that day up on Chinn Ridge. He hadn't known what was worse, the wound or the clumsy butchering of the army surgeon that meant he was never free of pain. And it was always worse at night. But it had been worth it. The bullet was his pass out of the sharpshooter units. He'd never seen

Major Kramer since the day he'd run out on his men. Ethan had lain in the sickbay tent, listening to the screams of the wounded and dying, slipping in and out of consciousness with pain and laudanum. He knew if he survived, he would go back to the regular ranks, but he was prepared to take his chances on the battlefield and die with honour rather than scurry about killing unarmed men on the orders of a coward.

'Wanna hug, Pa?' asked Lucy, cutting through his thoughts.

Ethan smiled. 'I sure could do with one.'

He reached out and Lucy climbed up onto his knees. As he wrapped his arms around her, she snuggled in close to his chest. They sat in silence as he gently rocked the chair, listening to the crickets and a dog barking somewhere out in the night.

'Will the bad dreams ever stop?' asked Lucy quietly.

'Don't know, baby. I don't know.'

'Ma knew how to stop them, didn't she?'

Ethan nodded. 'She sure helped.'

'I miss her.'

'I miss her too, darlin'.'

He gently kissed the top of her head, breathing in the smell of lavender from her hair. It was over a year now since Helen had died of tuberculosis but the simplest thing, like the scent of soap she used to make, still managed to remind him how raw his grief still was.

'You got the locket?' asked Lucy.

'You know I never take it off.'

He reached inside his shirt and pulled out the oval gold locket hanging from the end of its chain. He pushed on the side of it with his thumb and the lid sprang open. Inside was a tight curl of dark hair. He knew what was coming next.

'Tell me about the locket, Pa.'

'I must've told that story a thousand times. Don't you ever tire of hearin' it?'

'Nuh-uh.'

Ethan took a deep breath and hugged

Lucy a little tighter.

'Well, me and your ma hadn't been married all that long when I had to go and fight in the war. You were just a baby at the time.'

'She was the prettiest girl you ever saw, wasn't she?'

'She sure was. As pretty as you are now. Well, she made me promise I would come back to her. We had big plans. We were gonna live on a big farm, raise our pigs and have a platoon of kids. She gave me this locket and she made me swear on the Bible I would never take it off. She said it would keep me safe.'

'But you got hurt, didn't you?'

'Yes, I did. But it kept me alive. I'm in one piece, ain't I? Could've been a whole lot worse . . . '

'Ma was your guardian angel, wasn't she, Pa?'

'She sure was. Just the way she's lookin' over us now.'

The little girl smiled.

'Can I wear it for a little while?'

'Just for a little while.'

Ethan reached behind his neck, pulled the chain over his head and placed it over his daughter's. Lucy fell quiet as she inspected the locket but Ethan knew there was something else on her mind. Ethan rested his head back on the chair and closed his eyes. He knew she would get around to it eventually.

'Pa?'

'Mmm?'

'You thought 'bout tomorrow?'

'Yup. I thought about it.'

'So what do you think? Can we go? Everybody else is going. The whole school is goin'. They say there'll be fireworks. It's not every day a big important senator comes to a little place like Cotton Junction. Don't you want to see him? Hear what he's got to say?'

Ethan opened his eyes. 'Tell you the truth, darlin', there ain't much that politicians say that's got much to do with the likes of us. The only thing they care about is the vote. Senator Grimley and his like sent a lot of good men to an early grave for no good reason that I ever understood. Seems to me if they had to do the fightin', there'd be a lot less of it.'

Lucy listened quietly then snuggled into a tight ball and waited. Ethan smiled. She was so like her ma. She knew when to argue and when to wait for a better time.

It was true that Ethan had no time for politicians, but he knew that wasn't the whole reason for not wanting to go to Cotton Junction. When he came back from the war, he was a different man. Uneasy around people, he got panicky and broke out in cold sweats when he crossed the boundary of the homestead — as though something terrible might happen if he did. When Helen passed, that feeling only got worse. He only made the six-mile round trip to town when he really needed to. Once he had done their business and picked up their supplies, he didn't loiter.

Ethan knew it wasn't fair on Lucy. Apart from school and church, she was always with him. Ethan couldn't bear for her to be out of his sight. She never complained. She seemed to sense that she was needed; not just for the chores but to keep her pa safe from the nightmares that plagued him.

Ethan wished, for the millionth time, that Helen was here. It would all be so different. She would have made them all go to town. They would have packed a picnic and gone together on the buckboard, singing songs and making a great day of it.

But Helen wasn't here and Ethan knew he had to learn to be strong again on his own. For both of them.

'Lucy?'

'Yes, Pa?'

'About tomorrow?'

'Yes, Pa?'

'Let's take a picnic, shall we?'

Lucy jumped up as though a bee had stung her.

29

'Can we? Really? Can we go?' shouted Lucy, and threw her arms around his neck and gave him a tight hug.

'Hey, hey,' laughed Ethan, 'you're gonna choke the life out of me.'

'Thank you, Pa, thank you.'

'You'd better be gettin' to bed now. We got a busy day ahead of us. We'll need to get there early if we want a good view of the senator.'

Lucy burrowed down again.

'Just a little longer?'

'OK, then. Just for a little while,' smiled Ethan, and wrapped his arms around her.

'Tomorrow's gonna be a big adventure, ain't it, Pa?' said Lucy as she yawned and closed her eyes.

'A big adventure,' agreed Ethan as he gently rocked back and forth and knew he'd do anything for his little girl. He'd come back from Shiloh for her, hadn't he? And if he could do that, he could do anything. When Helen was dying, he had promised her he would take care of

Lucy. And that's what he intended doing. Even if he died trying.

It wasn't long before Lucy's breathing was deep and slow and, when he was sure she was sound asleep, Ethan gently lifted her and carried her through to the back of the shack where she slept in her cot. He lowered her down, pulled a blanket over her and pushed her dark hair, the same colour as her ma's, away from her eyes.

As he stood in the dark thinking about the day to come, he felt a sudden dread in the pit of his stomach.

He put his right hand out and spread his fingers. They trembled and shook as though they had a life of their own. Angrily he clenched them into a fist and thrust them into his pocket. With one last glance at Lucy, he went back out onto the porch and sat in his rocking chair, listening to the mournful whistle of a locomotive somewhere far out in the night heading in their direction.

2

Senator Ebenezer Grimley watched the moonlit Kentucky landscape pass as the locomotive ploughed through the sticky southern night. He rocked gently from side to side and puffed his thick cigar, enjoying his journey in this specially commissioned passenger car with its thick carpets, draperies and plush upholstered chairs. There were even separate cars for sleeping and dining in.

Very civilized, he thought to himself, someone should go into business making these things.

The senator was nearly sixty-five. He was short and plump with a full head of thick white hair and bushy whiskers to match, but he was a man still very much in his prime. No one had survived as long as he had in the dog-eat-dog world of Washington politics without a sharp intellect and the ability to judge a man's character and he was using both these faculties now as he listened to the heated argument between the two young men who shared his carriage.

Horace Crane, the senator's aide, was in his late twenties. He was lean-featured with intelligent dark eyes. His black, slicked-down hair gave him a bookish look and he had been educated in some of the best schools in Boston, but the senator recognized a ruthlessly ambitious man when he met one and knew that beneath the veneer of a polished gentleman, Crane had the instinct of a street-fighter. He was frequently grateful Crane's quick mind and sharp tongue were on his side.

The other young man in the carriage was George Laing. He was a detective with the Pinkerton Detective Agency. Senator Grimley hadn't had much time to get to know him since he had been a last-minute addition to the senator's entourage. After Lincoln's assassination, senior politicians had been given

33

protection — especially when travelling in the South.

George Laing was originally from Scotland and still had a strong Glaswegian accent that Grimley sometimes struggled to understand. He was the same age as Crane but thicker set, with honest blue eyes and, although not as well educated, was certainly no less sharp-witted. But he was quieter, less excitable than Crane. To Grimley it seemed he was always observing everything that went on around him, taking mental notes and filing them away for future use.

Although Crane had loudly resisted the notion of a personal bodyguard, Grimley instantly recognized Laing as a solid, dependable man who might prove useful in a tight spot, and had come round to the idea.

He wished the same could be said of his aide. The two young men mixed as well as oil and water and their initial distrust of each other was now openly hostile.

'Mr Laing, I really do not think that you have grasped the consequences of your advice,' Horace Crane was saying impatiently. 'It is imperative that the senator speaks at the rally at Cotton Junction tomorrow. There can be no question that he does not appear!'

'And I say it's too dangerous. Mr Lincoln's death has emboldened some rebel factions who believe they should never have surrendered. We have intelligence that indicates there may be other plots.'

'My job,' said Crane through clenched teeth, 'is to get the senator re-elected!'

'And my job, sir, is to ensure he does not die in the process!'

The senator sighed heavily. This argument had been going on between the two young men since dinner and, as the locomotive ate up the miles, the debate showed no sign of reaching a conclusion.

'Gentlemen, gentlemen,' said the senator eventually, rising from his chair with a groan, 'I am deeply indebted that both of you are so committed to my personal advancement and my protection, but we don't seem to be getting anywhere. I suggest we call it a night and sleep on it. With cool heads in the morning, I'm sure we'll be able to come up with a compromise that will satisfy us all.'

'Senator, with respect, sir,' said Crane, 'I do not think this matter can wait. There is still much preparation to be done for the rally. We can't just turn up at Cotton Junction. If this rally does not go smoothly, it would be most damaging to your campaign.'

Senator Grimley frowned, then sat back down with a sigh.

'Then let me make the decision for you, Mr Crane, otherwise I do believe the morning will find us all still sitting here.'

He looked at both young men in turn. He believed Laing. Pinkerton's intelligence was usually solid and if this young man thought there was a threat, then there probably was. In fact, there were many who believed that if the Pinkertons had been retained after the war as the president's personal body-guards, the assassination would not have happened.

On the other hand, Crane was right. If men were not free to assemble and speak then surely it was a betrayal of everything this great country had gone to war for?

'I am decided,' announced the senator, slapping his hands on his thighs. 'The rally will go ahead. I will speak at Cotton Junction tomorrow.'

Horace Crane could barely keep the smirk of victory from his face.

'However,' continued the senator, 'we'll postpone the event from the morning until noon. That will give Mr Laing the chance to scout around and ensure that everything is in order. If he comes with solid proof that it is not safe to proceed then we will not do so.'

'But, Senator . . . ' began Horace Crane.

The senator held up his hand to silence him.

'Have mercy, Mr Crane. I'm an old man. You two young bucks may want to sit up all night and spar, but as for me, I need some sleep.' He stood up. 'The matter is decided. I'll see you two gentlemen in the morning.'

There was a knock at the door. A smartly uniformed conductor entered, removing his peaked cap as he did so. The senator looked round.

'Yes, Mr Henderson? How can we help you?'

'Sorry to disturb you, Senator, but just to let you know we're approaching Juniper Creek. We're stopping to take on water and wood. We'll be there for an hour or so. You're welcome to get off and stretch your legs, but I'd advise you not to stray too far from the train.'

'Thank you, Henderson,' said the senator, flicking open his pocket watch, 'but as it's ten to midnight, I personally don't fancy strolling about in the dark. Goodnight, gentlemen.'

'Goodnight, sir,' said both men, as the senator left the room and made his way up the narrow corridor to the sleeping car, followed by the conductor.

An uneasy silence filled the room, broken only by the rhythmic click of the rails.

Eventually, Crane cleared his throat and stood up. 'I think I'll follow the senator's example and I, too, will retire for the night.'

As he reached the door, he stopped and turned. 'No hard feelings, I hope?' he said.

'None, whatsoever,' replied Laing, as he crossed his legs and lit a fresh cigar. Crane was about to say something, but thought better of it.

'Well, goodnight, then,' he said with a tight smile, and left the carriage.

★   ★   ★

As he closed the door behind him, the smile faded from Crane's face. He waited a few moments then made his way along the corridor through the sleeping car towards the conductor's car at the end of the train. He could hear the squeal of breaks as the train slowed on its approach to Juniper Creek.

As it came to rest with a loud gasp of escaping steam, he stepped out onto the plate at the back of the carriage and lowered himself down the steep stairs onto the rough wooden platform.

He waited, pulled out a thin silver case from his inside pocket and lit a small cigar. The two engineers had got out at the head of the locomotive and were checking wheels and oiling bolts. No one else got off the train and most of the carriages were in darkness. Even those that showed a light had blinds pulled down.

Crane patted the outside of his coat pocket and felt the solid outline of his derringer. Confident that no one had seen him, he walked slowly along the platform towards the stationmaster's office. He moved casually as though he was out for a stroll enjoying his cigar and the night air. When he was sure he couldn't be seen from the train, he started walking briskly towards the small group of buildings that made up Juniper Creek's main street. Everywhere was locked and in darkness but Crane quickly found the telegraph office and rapped impatiently on the small window. There was no reply. He rapped again a little louder, anxiously looking back towards the train, worried that he might be heard.

The shutter snapped up. A bleary-eyed face peered through the darkness at him.

'Were you not told to expect me tonight?' hissed Crane at the sleepy clerk.

'Thought you wasn't comin'. It's hellish late.'

'Never mind that,' snapped Crane. 'I need you to send a telegraph.'

'OK. Go ahead,' said the clerk, yawning as he pulled a pencil from behind his ear and licked the point.

'Send it to Cotton Junction.'

'What's the message?'

'WE CROSS THE RUBICON AT NOON.'

'That it?'

'That's it.'

'What in hell's name is a Rubicon?'

'You do not need to know!'

'OK,' said the telegraph clerk, making to close the window, 'I'll get this sent off first thing in the morning.'

Crane grabbed his wrist.

'No. Do it now!'

'Now? There won't be nobody to take it down at the other side!'

Crane smiled. 'I can assure you there will.'

'OK,' said the clerk, 'have it your way.'

Crane waited impatiently as the clerk tapped the message. After what seemed an age, he came back to the window.

'That's it. It's gone.'

'Good. Now give me the paper you wrote on.'

The clerk handed Crane the small pink form. He struck a lucifer, lit the bottom corner and watched as the paper flared. When it was black and twisted, he dropped it onto the sidewalk and twisted his boot on it. Satisfied, he turned to the clerk.

'Nobody must know about this message. Do you understand? This is government business. You know nothing. You've been paid well for your silence.'

'I knows it. Can I go back to bed now?' the clerk yawned.

'You may.'

The clerk snapped the window closed and Crane made his way back to the station.

The train stood in the moonlight, steam leaking from between its wheels, its engine occasionally hissing like a sleeping beast. The engineers were still busy and didn't notice Crane as he walked along the platform and hoisted himself back up into the carriage. He made his way along the corridor and stopped outside his berth.

'Thought you weren't coming back.'

Crane spun around, pulling the derringer out of his pocket. 'Mr Laing. What a surprise.'

'You always carry a gun, Mr Crane?'

'For the senator's protection.'

'You can put it away.'

'I thought you had retired,' said Crane, as he slipped the gun back into his pocket.

'I don't sleep much. Get what you need at the telegraph office?'

Crane's eyes narrowed. 'Have you been following me?'

'No, sir. Took a stroll, just like you did. Guess we went the same way.'

Crane stared at the detective, unsure if he was telling the truth. 'As a matter of fact, I did send the message I needed.'

'You always send telegraphs in the middle of the night?'

'It was concerning arrangements for tomorrow. As a government representative, I have access to the telegraph system whenever I need it.'

'You always burn them?'

'So you *were* following me.'

Laing said nothing.

'It was confidential, government business, Mr Laing.'

'So you say,' said Laing.

Crane took a step towards Laing until there was barely six inches between them.

'Mr Laing, I don't appreciate you spying on me. I think you are in real danger of overstepping your responsibilities and if you do, I will ensure your superiors are made aware of it.'

Laing smiled. 'I'll try to remember my place in future, Mr Crane.'

'Please do,' said Crane, his face flushing red with anger, as he opened the door to his berth. When he had closed the door behind him, he leaned against it and wiped the beads of sweat that had formed on his brow.

Laing was beginning to be a problem. Tomorrow at Cotton Junction, when it was all over, he would take great pleasure in wiping that smug smile off his face.

3

The morning of the rally was bright and warm and Ethan found he actually enjoyed the journey into Cotton Junction in the buckboard with Lucy. She chatted and sang the whole way and Ethan was glad he had decided to do this. He couldn't remember seeing her so happy.

The town was already busy by the time they arrived. Gaily coloured bunting was strung across the streets and a brass band played jaunty tunes while the crowds browsed the traders' stalls and shops that were all doing brisk business. There was a real carnival feeling about the place.

Ethan steered the buckboard into the livery stable and Lucy leapt down before the wheels had stopped turning.

'Can I go have a look outside, Pa?' she asked.

'Sure. But don't go far. Wait for me while I fix things here.'

Lucy started to run towards the large barn doors then stopped.

'I still got Ma's locket on. You want me to take it off?'

Ethan smiled. 'No, darlin'. You take care of it. Then I know you'll be safe.'

'Can I, Pa? Can I really?'

'Sure,' said Ethan, laughing. 'It looks better on you anyhow.'

Lucy threw her arms around his neck and kissed him on his cheek.

'Thank you, Pa. You're the best Daddy in the whole wide world!'

'Hey, you're gonna squeeze the life outa me. If you don't let me get with fixin' Buster, we ain't gonna see anything. Now git.'

'OK, Pa. Don't be long,' sang Lucy, as she ran out of the large barn doors into the bright, warm sunshine.

'And don't go far,' called Ethan, but she was gone. He smiled as he started unharnessing the horse.

'Long time no see, stranger.'

Ethan looked round.

'Well, Sheriff Winters! How the hell are you?' cried Ethan with a wide smile as he walked towards his old friend. They shook hands firmly. 'That badge sure does suit you.'

'Still getting used to it — and you don't have to call me Sheriff. I'm still Daryl to my friends.'

Lucy ran in through the doors and headed straight for Ethan. He swept her up in his arms.

'Hey, hey, what's the rush, young lady?' said Ethan.

'Pa! Pa! Can we go now? Can we?'

'Ain't you gonna show your manners and say hello to Sheriff Winters first? He's a big, important man now.'

Lucy slipped to the ground.

'Hello, Uncle Daryl.'

'Hey, Lucy. What's your daddy been feedin' you? You've sprouted up like a corn stalk since last I saw you.'

'It's been a while since you saw her, ain't it?' said Ethan.

'Too long since I saw both of you.

Last time was Helen's . . . '

A shadow passed over Ethan's face at the mention of his wife.

'Hey, why don't you back outside, Lucy. Don't go outside the corral, though. Don't wanna lose you.'

'"Bye, Uncle Daryl,' said Lucy as she ran back out into the sunshine.

'Sorry, Ethan,' Daryl began, 'didn't mean to open old wounds.'

'It's OK, Daryl. Not your fault. I guess I should be over it by now, but every time I hear her name . . . '

'That why you don't come to town anymore?'

'One of the reasons,' said Ethan, and then he forced a smile. 'Anyway, thought I'd bring Lucy in today and let her have some fun. Might even go to the rally and hear what the senator's got to say for himself.'

The band struck up a new tune and Daryl looked over his shoulder.

'Look, Ethan. I gotta go. I'm sort-of responsible for looking after the senator. You know, because of Lincoln and all, everybody's a bit skittish. I should be goin'. Got a lot on today.'

'You expectin' trouble?'

'Well, you know. Gotta be careful. Goes without sayin'. The senator ain't popular in these parts. The war's over but you know how it is. Lots of folks reckon we never should have surrendered, and they've got scores to settle. If they can get to Lincoln . . . '

'Well, don't let me hold you back, Sheriff. You got your duty to attend to.'

Daryl stretched out his hand again and smiled warmly. 'I'm mighty glad you came to town today, Ethan. Mighty glad. I'll be seein' you later.'

'Sure.'

When Daryl left, Ethan finished rubbing down his horse and made sure there was enough feed and water. He gathered up the pieces of tack and put them in the back of the buckboard and lifted out the picnic basket.

'Lucy!' he called. He checked on the horse one last time and patted him on the neck while he waited for Lucy to come bounding through the door.

'Come on, Lucy. Let's go!'

When Lucy did not appear for the second time, the first knot of worry began to tighten in the pit of his belly. It was that familiar feeling of dread he had felt the night before. He crossed to the door and looked into the corral where half-a-dozen horses were pacing around. Lucy was nowhere to be seen.

A stableboy was sitting on a barrel polishing a bridle.

'Hey, son, seen my kid around? Little girl. 'Bout eight. So high, dark hair, red-checked dress?'

'Yeah,' said the freckle-faced boy. 'I seen her. Was here about ten minutes ago. Went off with a fella. Thought he was her pa.'

'I'm her pa,' said Ethan, trying to keep the panic from rising in his throat. 'What'd this fella look like?'

'Didn't pay much attention. Tall. Might've been wearin' a uniform.'

'Which way they go?'

'Towards the station, I reckon.'

'Thanks, son. You see her again, you tell her I'm lookin' for her.'

'Sure thing, mister.'

Trying not to run, Ethan headed towards the centre of town. He kept telling himself there was an innocent explanation. She had met someone she knew. Maybe the teacher, or a neighbour, and although he was angry she had disobeyed him, he understood she was itching to meet her friends. He told himself not to be hard on her but there was still that knot in his belly.

The main street was packed with people. The band was playing loud. Flags flew from every building. As Ethan neared the station, he saw that a stage had been built in front of the platform. It was draped with yards of red, white and blue cloth and he guessed this was where Senator Grimley would address the crowd.

All the noise and colour began to be a blur as Ethan pushed his way through the crowds, craning his neck above their heads to see if he could see Lucy and the stranger she was with. He started to call her name but his voice was lost by the whistle of a locomotive as a train drew into the station. The crowd surged towards it and Ethan was jostled and shoved as he tried to make his way through them, like trying to swim against a river.

The knot of worry was now a ball of panic. The pressure of people pressing in on him began to make him sweat. His breathing was tight and shallow.

He pushed his way towards the sidewalk and standing on the steps he could now see across the heads of the mob.

'Lucy? Lucy?' he shouted, fear edging his voice. A couple of people turned to look at him. He grabbed their arms.

'You seen my little girl? I've lost her. She's only eight.'

They shook their heads and moved on. Ethan swept his hand across his hair and looked around him wildly. What was he to do? He grasped the handrail of the side walk and squeezed it tightly. He had to get a grip of himself and think!

Then behind him, he heard a voice he instantly recognized. It was quiet and friendly and it was a voice he hoped he would never have had to hear again as long as he lived.

'Lost something, Corporal van Kirk?'

Ethan swung around.

Leaning against the clapboard wall of the general store stood a tall, slim man with long, blond hair that fell to the shoulders of his beautifully tailored Confederate Army officer's uniform.

'Major Kramer . . . ?' whispered Ethan.

Kramer smiled widely, pushed off the building and walked towards Ethan.

'Somebody told me you was in town. Good to see you again, boy. Been a long time.'

Ethan stared at him, speechless.

'Imagine runnin' into you in this little place. What are the odds?'

'I . . . I . . . ' began Ethan.

Kramer put his hand on his shoulder.

'Tell you what. Why don't you come with me and I'll buy you a drink? You look as though you need one. We can catch up on old times — and there's somethin' I need to talk to you about.'

Ethan shook his head.

'I . . . I . . . can't. I'm lookin' for my little girl. She's gone off somewhere and . . .'

Kramer looked into Ethan's eyes and smiled. It froze Ethan's blood.

'Don't you worry 'bout Lucy. She's safe for now.'

Ethan felt as though he had been hit with a blacksmith's hammer.

'You know her? You know her name? How'd you . . . ?'

Kramer smiled, showing his impressive teeth.

'Sure, I know her. She sure is a pretty little thing. Now, come on, Corporal. You come with me and we can have our little talk.'

Kramer turned to walk along the

sidewalk. Ethan stood up straight and didn't move.

'Where is she, Kramer?'

Kramer stopped and turned.

'I told you, Corporal, she's safe. I need you to come with me so we can discuss a certain matter. It's important. So follow me.'

'I ain't talkin' to you 'bout nothin' until I get my little girl back. If you've laid one finger on her, so help me, I'll — '

'Now, now, Corporal van Kirk. You're in danger of bein' insubordinate to a superior officer.'

'Ain't you noticed? I ain't in the army no more — and you never were my superior.'

Major Kramer smiled. 'I understand. You're worried about your little girl. But you don't have to be. If you do what you're told.'

'I don't take orders from you anymore, y'hear?'

Kramer walked back towards Ethan until their heads were close. He spoke in a low voice. 'Corporal van Kirk. Let me spell this out for you. You will do *exactly* as I say if you ever want to see your daughter alive again. Do I make myself clear?'

Ethan felt a chill stab his heart. 'OK. I'll come with you,' he said in a whisper.

'That's better,' smiled Kramer. 'Glad you've seen sense, boy. Now, follow me.'

4

George Laing sat waiting pensively in a velvet-covered chair in the state room as the train slowly pulled into Cotton Junction. The brakes squealed in protest as they strained to bring tons of steel to a shuddering halt. After a few moments, Laing stood up and crossed to a window, lifted the blind and peered out.

As the train gasped its last breath of steam, the room filled with the sound of the noisy crowds outside and a brass band. He was deep in thought as the door opened and Senator Grimley entered, followed closely by Horace Crane.

'A very good morning to you, Mr Laing,' boomed Senator Grimley with a large smile.

'Good morning, sir.'

Crane said nothing, avoiding Laing's

eyes by pretending to rearrange some papers.

The senator looked Laing up and down, taking in his shadow of beard, crushed trousers and grimy collar. He cleared his throat as though he was about to break bad news to the detective.

'Laing, I . . . eh . . . hope you don't think me indelicate, but do you mind me asking you a question?

'Certainly not, Senator Grimley. How can I help you?'

'Have you, by any chance, been up all night?'

'Yes, sir. There were some matters I had to attend to.'

'You mean to say, you haven't slept at all?' asked the senator in amazement.

'Didn't you know, sir?' interrupted Crane, 'the Pinkerton Detective Agency has a motto. It is 'We Never Sleep'. Is that not so, Mr Laing?'

'That is indeed our motto,' replied Laing. 'That's how we catch criminals.'

'Very admirable, very admirable,'

chuckled the senator, 'and did you?'

'Did I what, sir?' asked Laing.

'Catch a criminal last night?'

Laing glanced at Crane.

'There was some suspicious activity, the details of which need not concern you until I fully understand their significance.'

'Activity?' asked the senator with some concern. 'What sort of *activity?*'

'Senator,' interrupted Crane before Laing could answer, 'it is a well-proven fact that lack of sleep can play tricks on tired minds, making people think there are schemes and plots which, in fact, do not exist.'

There was an uncomfortable silence as Crane and Laing glared at each other. The senator broke it by walking across to the window and looking out.

'Looks as though we have a great turnout, Crane,' he beamed.

'We have indeed, Senator.'

'So,' said Grimley, rubbing his hands together with enthusiasm, 'what is our plan for today?'

'As agreed last night,' said Crane, referring to the papers in his hand, 'you will make your main address to the crowd at noon. That will give everyone time to gather and by then they should all be in high spirits. There are correspondents from all the main newspapers coming and they will be here shortly before then. No point in having a triumphant rally if there is no one there to record it for posterity.'

'Absolutely, absolutely,' agreed the senator. 'Do you concur, Mr Laing?'

'That'll be fine, Senator. I'll have time to look around. Is there a sheriff in town?'

'I believe his name is Sheriff Daryl Winters,' said Crane, flicking through his sheaf of papers.

'I'll look for him.'

'We are agreed, then!' said the senator, eager to ease the frosty tension between the two men. He flipped open his pocket watch. 'It is now just before nine o'clock. That will give me plenty of time to go over this speech. We will reassemble here again at, say, eleven-thirty?'

Both men nodded in agreement.

'Excellent, excellent. Then I shall see you two gentlemen later.'

'Perhaps you should get some rest,' suggested Crane, when the senator had gone.

'I'll sleep when we're out of here with the senator safely on board.' Laing turned and looked out the window. 'There's something about this place that makes me uneasy.'

'I get the impression you are always uneasy, Mr Laing.'

'Sometimes it's just a gut feeling. But it's never let me down yet.'

Crane smiled.

'As you will, Mr Laing. Now, I have some people to meet and some final preparations to make, so I'll bid you good morning.'

Crane turned and left the room. He walked quickly along the corridor and then lowered himself down the steps onto the platform, noticing the half-dozen men spaced along it with rifles nestling in their arms and silver badges on their lapels. As he surveyed the milling crowds with satisfaction, Henderson approached him and handed him a folded piece of paper.

'Mr Crane, sir. I have a message for you.'

'From whom?'

'I don't know. A gentleman just came up and pressed this note into my hand and told me to give it to you.'

Crane looked at the letter. 'Did you read this?'

'Of course not, sir.' Henderson bristled at the slight.

'Well, thank you, anyway. You may go.'

The conductor scowled slightly as he touched the peak of his cap and walked away. Crane opened the folded paper and studied the hastily scribbled note.

There's been a change of plan. We have a room above a salon called

'Ruby's'. Come quickly.

Crane crushed the piece of paper in his hand. He didn't like changes of plan. He headed towards the steps to take him off the platform. In among the crowds, he asked a cowboy where he could find the saloon and headed in that direction. As he walked along the sidewalk, he turned into the first narrow alley he came to and, taking a lucifer from his pocket, scraped it against the wall. He lit the note. It flared quickly. As Crane dropped it to the ground, it shrank into a black, crumpled ball.

Satisfied the evidence was destroyed, he stepped back into the busy main street and walked along the sidewalk until he saw the sign for Ruby's and went through the batwing doors.

The piece of paper was still smouldering as George Laing entered the alleyway. He sniffed the air and looked down and saw the charred and blackened ball of ash. He squatted down to study it trying to gently prise open the tight curls of charred paper with his finger but they disintegrated under the lightest pressure.

'Damn,' he muttered, as he rose to his feet. He walked back out into the bright sunlight and looked at the saloon where Crane had gone. Why would someone like Crane go into a place like this? Laing considered following him in then decided against it.

Directly across from the saloon was a café with a bench outside. Laing went into it, ordered a coffee and then sat out on the sidewalk.

As his coffee cooled, he took out his pipe and a pouch of tobacco and settled down to see what Mr Horace Crane's next move would be. It seemed that, yet again, Laing's gut feelings were proving to be right.

5

In a daze, Ethan followed Kramer along the boardwalk, pushing their way through the crowds of people who loitered or strolled along the walkway. Many of the men held drinks, or smoked pipes, and the women were gossiping happily, carrying picnic baskets. Everyone, except Ethan it seemed, was enjoying their day out in Cotton Junction.

'In here.'

Kramer turned through the batwing doors of a saloon. Ethan looked up. The sign above said, Ruby's.

Out of the hot sun, the bar room was gloomy and cool. It was busy and Ethan noticed a few heads nodding in recognition towards Kramer. As they made their way to the bar, men stood aside to let him through.

'What'll it be, Major?' asked the barkeep.

'Two red-eye,' he said, without conferring with Ethan. As the two small measures were poured, a woman appeared behind the bar.

'Thought you'd got lost, Major,' she said.

'Hi, Ruby. I got distracted. Had to deal with a few things.'

The woman smiled warmly. Ethan reckoned she was about thirty or so. She had long brown hair which was pinned back on her head in a full, high bun. She had full sensuous lips and deep-brown eyes. Slim and well dressed, despite her femininity, she had a real presence and Ethan reckoned she didn't suffer fools for long. There were no other women in the bar but she was no soiled dove. She was dressed soberly in a modest grey dress and had a confident, assured presence that Ethan had never seen in a woman before. There was no doubt who was in charge.

The major threw back his glass and downed the whiskey in one gulp.

'Is he here yet?' he asked.

Ruby glanced at Ethan.

'It's OK,' murmured Kramer, 'he's with us.'

Ruby nodded towards the stairs at the back of the saloon that rose to a landing.

'He's upstairs. Got here a few minutes ago. Your sergeant's with him.'

'Good,' said Kramer, and then turned to Ethan. 'Drink up, boy. Got some people I'd like you to meet. See you later, Ruby.'

As Kramer headed towards the stairs, Ethan placed his untouched whiskey back on the bar. He looked directly at Ruby, wondering what part she had to play in all of this.

She nodded in Kramer's direction. 'You'd better go after him. He don't like bein' kept waitin'.'

Ethan followed Kramer up the wooden staircase. On the landing, they stopped outside the first room on their left. Kramer knocked on the door three times and waited. There were footsteps and then a booming voice in a broad Irish accent asked, 'Who is it?' The voice seemed vaguely familiar to Ethan but he didn't know why. Kramer put his head close to the door.

'It's me.'

Ethan heard the lock turn and then the door swung open. A large ruddy face with a patchy ginger beard and moustache looked out. The man wore an eye patch over his left eye and a large livid scar stretched down his face from his forehead to his chin. With a broad smile of recognition, he opened the door wide.

'Morning, Major,' he said, and stood back to let the two men into the room. The drapes had been drawn across the window and the only light was from two small kerosene lamps.

'Morning, Sergeant. All well?'

'No problems, sir,' boomed the Irishman. Ethan stared at the large man in disbelief.

'What's wrong, Corporal? You look as though you've seen a ghost!'

'Sergeant Finnegan? Is it you?' said Ethan in a whisper.

''Course it's me!' The Irishman grasped Ethan's hand and shook it warmly. 'This is like old times. It's great to see you, laddie.'

Ethan could hardly speak. Eventually he managed to gasp, 'But you . . . I saw you killed . . . that day up on Chinn Ridge . . . '

'Ah, that was a close thing.' He touched the large scar on his cheek. 'Cost me an eye and I ain't ever gonna be the handsomest man in the room.'

'How did you . . . ?'

'How did I survive? Just lay and didn't move. After you made your leap off the cliff, them Yankee bastards left us for dead. But it was you they were after. They got on their horses and were off like bats out of hell trying to find a way down to the river to get you. The other two had died but I lay there until nightfall then started to crawl. Next day I got picked up by a Yankee patrol and sat out the rest of the war as a guest of

Abe Lincoln. They let me go 'bout three months after the war ended.'

Ethan stared at the sergeant. 'I don't believe it . . . '

'If you two gentlemen are finished with your reunion, we got business to attend to. Take a seat, Corporal.'

For the first time, Ethan looked around.

The room was furnished with a double bed with a patterned throw. There was a small, round table and a couple of chairs by the window. On the table was a china coffee pot with two fine cups and saucers that looked strangely out of place. He glanced around quickly, looking for Lucy.

'Where's my kid?'

Kramer sat at the table and pulled out a cigar. He bit off the end and spat it out.

'All in good time, Corporal, all in good time. There's someone I want you to meet first.'

Ethan hadn't noticed another door which led to a side room. As Kramer spoke, it opened and a dapper young man emerged. He nodded at Kramer, and then looked at Ethan. As he dried his hands with a linen towel, Ethan could smell some sort of fancy cologne. The young man smiled broadly as he walked towards Ethan and offered his hand.

'Corporal van Kirk, I presume?'

Ethan shook the proffered hand.

'It's just plain mister. Ain't been a corporal for quite a while now.'

'Well, Mr van Kirk, allow me to introduce myself. My name is Crane. Horace Crane.'

6

'Having another, Mayor O'Neil?' asked Ruby.

The gentleman in the black frock coat had been standing at the bar for half an hour, nursing his glass of red-eye. He looked like a man who had somewhere to go but didn't want to leave the saloon.

'I'd better not, Ruby. I'm sharing the stage with the senator in a few hours.'

'Thought you'd be there already, what with you being the mayor and all.'

The mayor shook his head.

'Seems I'm not required. I've been told everything is in hand. Sheriff Winters is looking after the senator along with some posh fella he brought from Washington. Crane, I think they said his name is. Besides, seems there's been a change in plans. He's not speaking until noon so I thought I'd use the time wisely in my favourite saloon with my fellow citizens.'

Ruby smiled at the mayor. He was an old lawyer and had decided to run for mayor five years ago and he had won the election every year since. With his unruly grey hair and untidy suit, some people might have underestimated him until you looked into his piercing, grey eyes that sparkled with intellect. He had made a lot of changes to Cotton Junction, all of them good in Ruby's opinion and she couldn't imagine anyone filling his shoes any time soon.

'How about you, Abe?' said Ruby, to the thin man standing next to the mayor. Abe Skinner owned the biggest general store in the area and had done pretty well for himself. But now that he had tasted success in business, he wanted success in politics and had been Mayor O'Neil's closest rival in the last election.

'Don't mind if I do, Ruby,' he said, offering his empty glass across the bar.

'I ain't been invited to the stage — but then I ain't as important as our mayor here so I guess I'll just have to listen to the senator from the cheap seats same as most everyone else.'

'Could be you next year, Abe,' said O'Neil. 'This year's election was a close-run thing. Could be you having to do all this important stuff like listening to some old wind bag from Washington wastin' a good dinner. You jist be careful what you wish for. Right now, I'd gladly change places with you.'

Abe turned round to face the older man.

'That's the thing about you, O'Neil. Why'd you keep running for mayor if you don't want the job? Why not just stand aside and let someone in who really wants to do it?'

Mayor O'Neil placed two hands on the bar and turned his head to look at the younger man straight in his eyes.

'Because I'm better at it than you,' replied the old man. 'I know you want the job badder than a baby wants a teat

75

but you want it for all the wrong reasons.'

'Now jist you wait a minute, there — '

'You want the big office and the fancy dinners and all those people who come out of the woodwork to tell you just what a great guy you are now you've got a bit of influence. The kind of men who, before you were mayor, wouldn't have spat on you if you were on fire. I don't blame you. For a while, that's kinda nice. But it soon wears off, believe me. And the stuff you're left with — the important stuff — is just a daily grind tryin' to do what's right for this town. Until I find a man who wants the job because he wants to do right by the people of Cotton Junction and not because of all the worthless trinkets that go along with it, I'm stayin' put!'

'Hey, it's like the election all over again,' laughed Ruby. 'Don't look so hurt, Abe. It ain't personal. It's only politics, ain't it, Mayor?'

Mayor O'Neil emptied the last of his

red-eye and winked at Ruby.

'That's right, Ruby. It's only politics.'

Their conversation was suddenly drowned out by the crash of glass and a roar from the corner of the saloon. There were two cowboys rolling on the floor with cards and coins all around them.

'Excuse me, gents,' said Ruby.

She lifted a section of the bar and almost ran across to the fight. A circle of men had surrounded them, egging them on, but Ruby pushed through the crowd easily. She grabbed the cowboy on top by the scruff of the collar and pulled him off the man he was punching, who was probably too drunk to feel a thing.

'All right, you two. Break it up! There'll be no brawlin' in my bar. You can take it outside and finish it if you like but not under my roof!'

One of the cowboys, an older 'puncher in his forties, looked sheepish.

'Sorry, ma'am. Things got a little outa hand,' he said as he lifted his hat.

He turned to the younger cowboy he had been fighting. 'You want me, I'll be outside.'

He touched the brim of his hat towards Ruby and walked out of the bar.

'What you waitin' for?' said Ruby to the younger cowboy.

'I ain't leavin' on account of no woman,' he said, looking at her with disdain. 'Anyhow's, I'm gonna pick up my winnin's that that no good skunk was tryin' to cheat me out of.'

Ruby put her hands on her hips and looked up at the young man. He was a good foot taller.

'Is that right? Well, I reckoned on keepin' the money. I don't care who you say it belongs to but it'll cover the cost of these chairs and tables you two have broken. And as for leavin', you ain't got no choice. I own this place. You got thirty seconds to get your butt out of my sight before I take you outside myself and teach you a lesson in manners you'll never forget.'

The cowboy looked at her in disbelief. He had never been spoken to like that before by anyone — let alone a woman. He looked around at the grinning faces all around him and knew he had talked himself into a corner. He looked cheap picking up money off the floor and he looked a coward talking about fighting a woman. Cotton Junction could still be a rough town but striking a woman just wouldn't be tolerated. He knew if he made a single move towards her, these men around him would shoot him where he stood.

'Well? I'm a'waitin',' said Ruby with her hands on her hips and tapping her toe impatiently on the floor.

'I'm goin'. You can keep the money . . .' murmered the boy, as he put his hat back on and walked towards the batwings. A chorus of laughter and ridicule followed him and Ruby knew he would never show his face in her saloon again.

She went back to the bar.

'Can you get that mess cleaned up, Walter?' she said to one of the barkeeps.

'Sure thing, Miss Ruby,' he said, grabbing a broom, grinning from ear to ear. 'Now, where were we, gentlemen, before we were rudely interrupted?'

Mayor O'Neil was smiling too.

'I was just tellin' Mr Skinner here about the type of mayor we need in Cotton Junction. Someone able, strong-minded and not afraid of standin' up for themselves. You ever decide to run for office, Ruby, you'd get my vote. What'd you say, Abe?'

Abe Skinner said nothing and drank the rest of his whiskey.

'Thanks for the drink, Ruby,' O'Neil said. 'Well, nearly ten o'clock. Best be goin' and gettin' ready for the senator. Reckon I got myself a lot of kissin' babies and shakin' hands to do.'

7

Ethan didn't trust a man with a weak handshake.

'Pleased to meet you, Mr Crane,' Ethan said as he felt his smooth, limp hand in his. 'I don't mean to be discourteous but the only reason I'm here is to pick up my little girl. So if you just let me have her, I'll be on my way.'

Crane nodded, then walked over to the table.

'Coffee?' he said, offering one of the fine, bone-china cups.

'Not for me,' said Ethan.

'Do you mind if . . . ?' said Crane, pointing to the coffee pot.

'Go right ahead.'

Crane sat down, crossed his legs neatly and began to pour. He held the lid of the coffee pot with one finger and when he had finished, he tipped in milk from a small pot and lifted two spoonfuls of sugar from a bowl.

'I like my coffee the European way,' he said, sitting back and stirring slowly, all the while looking at Ethan with interest. Eventually he tapped the spoon against the cup and placed it carefully in the saucer.

'So, Corporal van Kirk, I take it you have no idea why you are here?'

'I'm here to get my little girl back. Kramer says he knows where she is.'

'Indeed. I can confirm we have your child and she is perfectly safe.'

Ethan felt a fury rise in his chest. 'Then I want her back and I want her back now,' he said as calmly as he could.

Crane nodded. 'Of course. I understand your concern. She will be returned to you just as soon as you have completed your mission successfully.'

'My mission?' spat Ethan. 'What d'you mean, *my mission?* You take my child and then you start givin' me orders. Why, I oughta — '

Ethan lunged at Crane, his fists raised. He had hardly taken one step forward when he felt his arms pinned to his side as Finnegan grabbed him.

'Now, now, laddie,' said Finnegan in his ear.

'Get your hands offa me, you big Irish piece of horse-shit.' Ethan swung his heel behind him to catch his shins but Finnegan, veteran of many bar-room brawls, easily stepped aside. He spun Ethan round quickly and sank a fist into his ribs. Ethan dropped to the floor, gasping for breath. He felt a boot push him onto his back. Crane, still holding his coffee cup, looked down on him.

'Now listen to me, Corporal. We have little time for theatricals. I need you to pay attention. We have your daughter and make no mistake: we will kill her if you do not do as we ask. Of course, you don't know me and you may wish to call my bluff, thinking I would never go through with my threat, but you know Major Kramer and Sergeant Finnegan and you know that they would.'

'What do you want from me?' Ethan hissed, looking up at Crane with hatred blazing in his eyes.

'That's more like it,' smiled Crane as he sat back at the table. 'Please, sit on the bed. You'll be more comfortable.'

'Get him on the bed,' said Kramer.

Finnegan lifted Ethan off the floor as though he was a rag doll and threw him on the bed. Ethan let out a low groan as he clutched his ribs. He felt as if he had been kicked by a mule.

'Now,' said Crane, 'Major Kramer tells me you were one of his best sharpshooters during the war. Is that correct?'

'He was,' confirmed Kramer.

'Well, we have need of your skills again,' said Crane.

'I don't understand,' mumbled Ethan, still holding his ribs.

'You know that Senator Grimley from Washington will be speaking to the good citizens of Cotton Junction today at noon. He will address them from the stage at the railway station.'

'What's that got to do with me?'

Crane took a sip of his coffee and smiled.

'Your mission is to kill him.'

At first, Ethan thought he had heard him wrong. Then he started to laugh.

'You want me to kill a United States senator? You must be out of your mind.'

'I'm glad you find it so amusing but I've never been more serious in my life.'

'You're crazy. You're all crazy. I'm not going to kill nobody for nobody.'

'One last time — '

'Even if I wanted to, I can't! Look at me . . . '

Ethan held out his hands. Even in the gloom, they could see the tremor that caused his fingers to vibrate.

'I can't,' Ethan whispered. 'This is what the war did to me. Me and hundreds of others. My nerves are shot.'

'I'm sure once you get a gun back in your hands, it'll all come back to you,' said Crane evenly.

Ethan shook his head. 'I can't do it. I *won't* do it!'

There was an uneasy silence in the room. Ethan looked from man to man. They watched him, stony-faced. Eventually Crane spoke.

'Don't you think it's a fair deal?'

'What is?'

'The life of the senator for the life of your child.'

Ethan stared at Crane.

'What kinda deal is that? It's the Devil's deal.'

'It may well be so, but it's the only one that's on the table.'

Ethan said nothing. After a few moments, Crane turned to Kramer.

'Major Kramer, I'm beginning to think this has been a big mistake. This man is obviously not suitable for the task.'

'That's what I've been trying to tell you!' said Ethan.

'But he knows too much now,' continued Crane. 'Take him and his brat and get rid of them both.'

Kramer nodded and stood up.

'Wait!' shouted Ethan.

'Change of heart, Mr van Kirk?'

Ethan put a hand to his head. 'Let me think . . . I need to think . . . '

Crane took out a silver pocket watch from the waistcoat of his dark suit. 'You have exactly sixty seconds to make up your mind.'

'Why?' shouted Ethan. 'Why me? Why're you doin' this to me?'

No one answered him. Outside, the noisy crowd's yelling and laughter mixed with the music from the band. Raucous singing had started in the saloon below, but all Ethan could hear was the ticking of Crane's watch. He heard each second go by and prayed that this was some kind of nightmare from which he would wake up. But he didn't. And it wasn't.

Ethan looked at the three men in turn. They were mad, of that there was no doubt, but they were serious and determined in their madness. The only thing he could do was buy time until he figured a way out.

'I'll do it,' said Ethan quietly.

Crane smiled at Kramer. 'Excellent. Well, now that that's settled you will have to excuse me, gentlemen. I need to get back to the senator to ensure he appears at the appointed hour. I trust you will all be equally diligent in playing your part in the successful outcome of our endeavour.'

He lifted the fragile coffee cup, his little finger extended, and drank the remainder of his coffee.

'Good day, gentlemen,' he said, and without a backward glance, left the room.

8

George Laing sat on the wooden bench outside the cafe, packing tobacco into his pipe, deep in thought. His gaze was fixed on the batwing doors of Ruby's saloon directly across the street as he made a mental note of every man who went in and, more importantly, every man who came out.

Reaching into the waistcoat of his crumpled brown suit, he pulled out a lucifer and scratched it against the leg of the bench. He offered the flame to the pipe's bowl and started to draw deeply. As the flame flared and guttered out, Laing leaned back and blew large blue clouds of smoke above him. To any passer-by, he looked a contented man, without a care, sitting in the shade, sipping coffee, smoking his pipe and enjoying the happy festival mood of the town. They couldn't have been more wrong. Laing felt he had the weight of the world on his shoulders as he flipped open his pocket watch and glanced down.

'Ten o'clock,' he murmured to himself.

He looked up at the sun as if checking the timepiece was telling the truth before tipping his dusty bowler a little more forward over his eyes and settling back to wait. Waiting didn't bother him. He was a patient man. He knew by experience that most of a detective's work was dull and routine. Sifting papers, gathering evidence, tailing people. The attribute Alan Pinkerton most prized among his detectives was dogged patience.

But Laing knew time was against him if he was going to prove to the senator he was in grave danger. As yet, all he had was the sinking feeling in the pit of his belly.

He knew Crane was up to something and, despite all his big talk, Laing knew he didn't have the senator's best interests at heart.

From the first time they had met, three days ago in Washington, Crane had made it very clear he didn't want Laing anywhere near the senator. Laing had just put it down to professional defensiveness. He had made it obvious from the start that he saw the Pinkerton detective as unnecessary and perhaps even a slight on his own ability to protect the senator. Laing could understand that. Maybe in Crane's boots he would have felt the same way. But that didn't explain everything; there were too many unanswered questions.

Why did Crane go sneaking off in the night like that if it was official business? Why burn the telegram and the message in the alleyway? And what was the message he sent and who received it?

But the thing that nagged at Laing most was why Crane was so determined to get the senator to speak at Cotton Junction today. Laing understood it was important for the senator to be seen in the South but this was only one place of a hundred he could have done it. Why *this* place? And why *now?*

Laing puffed on his pipe with frustration and looked over at the busy saloon. Here was yet another thing that didn't fit. What was a man like Crane doing in a place like Ruby's? Sure, it wasn't the worst doggery he'd seen but it certainly wasn't the kind of place a Boston gentleman with political connections would frequent. Laing knew every man had his weakness whether it was liquor, women, money or power, sometimes all of them. What was Crane doing in there? And who was he with?

He looked at his watch again. Time was marching on and the senator would be expecting Crane to be back on the train helping him put his finishing touches to his speech. Laing felt a pang of panic and sat forward on the bench. Had he missed Crane? Had he slipped out of the saloon unnoticed? Laing considered heading back to the train, but, just as he was about to rise, the batwings swung open and Horace Crane stepped out into the sunshine.

Laing sat back again, hoping Crane hadn't seen him. Crane looked up and down the street and then started to make his way along the sidewalk towards the train. When he had a few dozen yards' head start, Laing slowly rose and started to follow him, matching his pace to maintain the distance between them.

As Crane neared the station, Laing stopped on the corner outside the telegraph office. He watched as Crane meandered through the crowds and up onto the platform. He spoke to no one as he boarded and disappeared into one of the carriages.

Laing knocked the ash from his pipe against the wall of the telegraph office. The more he thought about it, the more he was sure the key to all of this was the message that Crane had sent last night from Juniper Creek — if he could just get a hold of it. The only chance there might be of that happening was to get the boys back in Denver onto it. Maybe they could track it down. But it would take a while. Laing knew there was no chance of getting the message today, but at least he would have set the wheels in motion.

He glanced at his watch again. It was 10.25. He snapped it shut then turned into the office to see if he could find out any more about the mysterious Mr Crane and the messages he didn't want anyone to know about.

9

Ethan followed Kramer down the stairs into the saloon to a corner table, away from the rowdy poker and faro games. Ruby was standing at the end of the bar and Kramer nodded at her, indicating for her to come over. Then he turned to Ethan as they sat down.

'I know it's a lot to take in, boy, but it'll make sense soon enough. Just do what we ask and you can get your kid and go home.'

'What I don't understand is, why?'

'Why, what?'

'Why you want the senator dead?'

Kramer sighed and looked around him then leaned across the table, speaking in a low voice.

'Grimley and his like think they won the war. They didn't. We just gave up too soon.'

Ethan stared at Kramer but didn't say anything.

'You don't believe me?' said Kramer.

'You forget, I was there. They had us licked.'

Kramer smiled. 'That's what they want you to believe. You been reading too many northern newspapers.'

'Nobody thinks we coulda won the war.'

'You're wrong, boy,' said Kramer, shaking his head. 'There's a lot of people think we could've turned the tide — and they're just waiting for a signal to rise up again!'

'What sorta signal?'

'Like a senior politician gettin' gunned down. That could spark things off.'

'What about Lincoln? He got killed. I didn't see no war breakin' out. Why didn't all these folks you say there is rise up then?'

'It was too early. Booth was working on his own. We weren't organized.'

'And you are now?'

Kramer nodded slowly and smiled. 'We're ready.'

'Are you the leader?'

Kramer laughed. 'No, I'm way down the peckin' order. I got a role to play, what with my military experience, but there's far more important than me involved in this. It goes all the way to the top — and I mean all the way. Yessir, things'll be different next time.'

'Next time? What do you mean, next time?'

'When we're at war again.'

Ethan felt dizzy with shock as though all the blood had drained from his head.

'You wanna start a war again?' he almost whispered. 'Why, in the name of God?'

Kramer looked at him like a child struggling with simple math.

'We were sold out, Corporal. We didn't need to surrender!'

'Jesus Christ, Kramer. You were there. You saw it. How many more men have got to die? Wasn't a couple of hundred thousand enough for you the first time around?'

Ethan looked deep into Kramer's grey eyes. They were as cold and cunning as a wolf's.

'I don't expect you to understand, Corporal. War can do different things to men. Some get a bellyful, some snap under the strain of it. Others, they can't get enough of it. I guess that's me.' Kramer leaned forward and lowered his voice so no one else could hear. 'Let me tell you something I have never told another soul, Corporal. When we were at war, in amongst all that killin' and dyin' and sufferin', it was the one time in my life I felt truly *alive*.'

Ethan stared at Kramer and wondered if it was the face of a madman. They sat looking at each other in silence until Ethan realized Ruby was standing next to them.

'You two gentlemen drinkin' or you both just gonna sit there gassin' like a couple of old women?'

Kramer sat back in his chair and

laughed loudly, the moment of madness gone.

'Whiskey. Bring the bottle,' said Kramer, as though he and Ethan were just two old comrades catching up on old times.

'Sure thing,' said Ruby and crossed to the bar.

Kramer put a boot on the empty chair across from him.

'You'll be fine, Corporal. A strong drink'll stiffen your nerve and you'll be ready for action again.'

Ethan shook his head.

'I told you, Kramer. You've picked the wrong man. After what happened up on Chinn Ridge and then Shiloh . . . I guess I'm one of those who got more'n a bellyful of killin'.'

'Think of your little girl. That'll keep you motivated, Corporal.'

'Stop callin me *Corporal*,' said Ethan quietly. 'I ain't in the army no more. Don't you understand? The war is *over*!'

'Just because the war is over, don't

mean the fightin' is,' said Kramer, glaring at him.

Ethan glared at Kramer and realized he was wrong; he *could* kill again. If he had had a gun in his hand right at that moment, he would have placed the barrel to Kramer's head and not thought twice about blowing his brains out.

'Ah, here's our drinks,' said Kramer, as Ruby arrived carrying a tray with a bottle of whiskey and two glasses. 'Pour this man a drink, Ruby. I'll be back in a minute. Need to go speak to Finnegan about something.'

Kramer left Ethan sitting at the table and went upstairs. Ruby uncorked the bottle and poured two shots. She looked at Ethan closely as she poured.

'What's up, mister? You OK?'

Ethan didn't reply. He reached out for the glass. Drops of whiskey slopped over the side as he tried to steady his trembling hands. He quickly drank the amber liquid and felt its sharp burn down his throat.

'Pour me another, will ya?'

'You'd better take it easy with this stuff, Soldier,' said Ruby, as she refilled his glass.

Ethan looked up at her. Her eyes were a deep, liquid brown and although her smile was warm and friendly, it failed to hide the deep sadness in them.

'How do you know Kramer?' asked Ethan.

'The major? My husband was in one of his units during the war.'

'Was?'

'He didn't make it. Killed at Shiloh.'

'I was there. It was hell.'

'So they say,' said Ruby quietly, and turned to leave. Ethan reached across and grabbed her wrist.

'Don't go. Sit a while.'

'I gotta get back . . . '

'Please. I could do with the company.'

'Listen, mister, this ain't that kind of a place. If it's company you're lookin' for — '

'No, it ain't that. I just need to . . .

101

talk to someone.'

Ruby looked doubtful then said, 'Well, OK — but just until the major gets back.'

As she sat down beside him, Ethan could smell the faint scent of lavender and he noticed how a loose curl of hair fell from behind her ear and rested on her smooth, white neck. Ethan realized she was the first woman he had looked at like this since his wife had died.

'I fought with Kramer, too.'

'He's a good man.'

'Is he? I used to think that. There was a time I would've followed him into hell.'

'And now?'

'I think he just dragged me into it.'

'What d'you say?'

'Nothin'.'

Ethan decided to take a risk. He sat forward in his chair and looked around to make sure no one was watching.

'Look, Ruby, I don't know you but you seem like a decent person. You got kids?'

'That's a personal question, Mr — '

'Van Kirk. Ethan van Kirk. I'm sorry. I didn't mean to pry.'

'No, I don't have kids. We always wanted them but . . . '

'I got a kid. The most beautiful little girl you ever saw. Lucy's her name.'

'I'm happy for you.'

Ethan reached across and grasped Ruby's hand. She made to pull away.

'Ruby, I need help. I don't know who to turn to.'

'Whatever sort of trouble you're in, you can tell the major.'

'No!'

A couple of card players nearby looked round and Ethan realized he had raised his voice. He looked towards the stairs. He had to tell Ruby everything before Kramer came back.

'Kramer has got my daughter.'

'He's what?'

'Listen. He's got my little girl. He's gonna kill her if I don't do something for him.'

Ruby tried to pull her arm away.

'You sure you're all right, mister? You don't look so good.'

'He wants me to kill the senator. If I don't, he's gonna kill my daughter. I think she's upstairs in that room they have. You gotta help me!'

Ruby stared at Ethan for a few moments and then smiled. She gently prised his fingers open and then patted the back of his hand kindly.

'Listen, mister. I got that room ready myself. There's no kid up there. Major Kramer just wanted a room for a few hours for a place to meet. You got it all wrong. He's not gonna hurt the senator, he's here to *protect* him. Told me himself. Said he was goin' to get some of the old boys together for one last mission. I thought you was one of 'em.'

'No, Ruby . . . it's not that way at all.'

'Now hush, mister. No point gettin' yourself into a lather 'bout nothin'. I know you must have gone through hell and back. I can see it in your eyes. I've seen how some other fellas came home from the fightin' — a lot worse'n you — their nerves all shot to pieces, twitchin' and stammerin'. You just need to get yourself some rest. Now, you just sit there quiet and have your drink and I'll tell Major Kramer all about it.'

'Tell me what?'

Ethan and Ruby looked up. Kramer was standing over them.

'What've you two been talkin' about?'

Ethan froze. He stared across the table at Ruby. She smiled up at Kramer.

'Why, we were talkin' about you, Major.'

Ethan felt his fingers grip the edge of the table.

'What about?' said Kramer, eyeing her suspiciously.

Ruby looked at Ethan then turned back to Kramer.

'Mr van Kirk was just tellin' me he served with you during the war.' She stood up and pushed her chair in to the table. 'He was just sayin' what an honour it was to serve under you.'

'That right?' said Kramer, staring at Ethan.

'He sure was. Anyway, I'll leave you two gentlemen to get on with your business. Good day, Mr van Kirk.'

Ethan watched her turn and go back to the bar.

She hadn't believed him.

Nobody would.

10

George Laing pushed open the glass-fronted door of the telegraph office and above his head a small bell on a spring rang cheerfully. A balding clerk with a green visor on his forehead looked up from behind the wooden counter with a friendly smile.

'Good morning, sir. What can I do for you?'

'Need to send a telegraph. It's urgent.'

'That's what we're here for,' beamed the clerk. 'Just jot down your message here, sir, and I'll have it gone in no time.'

He passed Laing a pink Western Union form and offered him a pencil. As Laing began to write, he found the clerk staring at him.

'Something you want to ask?'

'I'm sorry, sir, but I was just

wondering. That wouldn't happen to be a Scottish accent, would it?'

'Aye. It is.'

'Glasgow or thereabouts, if I'm not mistaken?'

'It is indeed. The Gorbals. How did you know?'

'My mother, Mary McLaren, was from Glasgow. Always good to meet someone from the 'auld' country.' He thrust his hand over the counter. 'Andrew Nesbitt's the name.'

Laing shook his hand. 'George Laing. Glad to meet you, Nesbitt.'

'Likewise.'

'Now,' said Laing, indicating the form, 'if you don't mind, I really have to — '

'Of course, of course. Go right ahead.'

Laing finished the message which read:

THE PINKERTON DETECTIVE AGENCY, DENVER, NEED INFORMATION ON A TELEGRAPH SENT

YESTERDAY AT MIDNIGHT FROM JUNIPER CREEK. STOP. SENDER WAS HORACE CRANE. STOP. URGENT THAT CONTENTS ARE KNOWN. STOP. MATTER OF NATIONAL IMPORTANCE. STOP.

He quickly checked over what he had written then handed it over to the telegraph operator. When he had read its contents, the smile faded from Nesbitt's face.

'You're a Pinkerton man?' he whispered.

Laing looked behind him. The telegraph office was empty.

'Aye. I am. But I'd appreciate it if that fact was kept just between ourselves.'

'Of course, sir, of course,' said the clerk. He tapped the side of his nose. 'Discretion is our watchword.'

'Glad to hear it.'

'Matter of national importance, you say?'

'I'm afraid it is. So the sooner it gets

sent, the better.'

'And will you wait for a reply?'

'I can't. I need to get on. I don't think they'll have the answer for me within a few days anyway.'

'But if it is a matter of national importance — '

'This information is crucial but I don't see how I can get the answer any quicker.'

'I see . . . ' said the clerk thoughtfully. 'National importance . . . ' He seemed to like the gravitas of the phrase.

Laing nodded, watching him.

'It wouldn't happen to involve, by any chance, the senator's visit today?' asked the clerk.

'It might.'

The clerk tapped his teeth with the end of his pencil and studied the note again as though he was solving some cryptic puzzle.

'You know, Mr Laing, I just might be able to help.'

'How so?'

'Now this is highly irregular and if

word gets out I could lose my job.'

'I guarantee no one will know.'

'And since you're a fellow Scot — '

'We could be related,' smiled Laing.

'Well, the thing is,' said the clerk, indicating Laing to come closer, 'I know Albert Feeney.'

'Who's Albert Feeney?' asked Laing.

'Albert is the telegraph operator at Juniper Creek. Instead of going all this long way round via Denver and then our offices and all its beaurocracy, why don't I just wire Albert and ask him what the message was and where he sent it to? I mean, it's against every regulation in the book but . . . '

'Would he do it, this Albert Feeney?'

The clerk smiled. 'Let's say he owes me a favour. There's a young lady he sometimes comes to Cotton Junction to see whom I don't think his wife would approve of, if you know what I mean?'

Laing smiled. 'I do.'

'And if it's a matter of national security . . . '

'It certainly is,' confirmed Laing.

'Then wait here and I'll see what I can do.'

As the clerk bent to his task, Laing walked over to the window and watched the crowds stream by as he listened to the gentle clack of the telegraph hammer. As he waited, Laing surveyed the buildings that lined the busy main street and wondered how he could protect the senator against someone determined to do him harm. He quickly came to the conclusion, it was impossible. Too many people. Too many two- and three-storey buildings with windows overlooking the railway and the platform. If it were me, thought Laing, I'd put a sharpshooter up there. But that was just one method. It could just as easily be a pistol from close range or explosives under the platform.

He surveyed the buildings again, the rows of stores and offices. One store front caught his eye. The windows were empty of merchandise and the glass was covered in dust.

Nesbitt came back to the counter.

'That's the message sent. Shouldn't be long comin' back to us.'

'I appreciate this,' said Laing.

The clerk waved his hand. 'Think nothing of it.'

Laing pointed out the window. 'I was just standin' here wonderin' about that empty store over there. Somebody own it?'

The clerk followed his gaze.

'Old Wiseman's place? Been boarded up for months now. Used to be a tailor's. Had a great goin' business there too, then all of a sudden, Wiseman tells me he got an offer for it he couldn't refuse. Wouldn't go into any details. Said he couldn't. Just sold up and left town. Never heard from him again. The shop's been lying empty ever since, though I reckon I get asked about it twice a day. Good store fronts are hard to get in Cotton Junction.'

The detective pondered the store a little longer then, as usual, filed the information away, feeling it was significant but not really knowing why.

He checked his watch every minute. He couldn't afford to wait much longer and he was about to tell the clerk to bring the message to him as soon as he got it, when the hammer on the telegraph started to rise and fall. No matter how often he had seen it, Laing never got used to this new-fangled technology.

The clerk hastily scribbled down the message. Eventually the tapping stopped and he handed over the sheet of paper triumphantly.

'Here you go. Whadya know? The message was sent to this office. It's for the attention of a Major Kramer.'

Laing read the words carefully three or four times.

WE CROSS THE RUBICON AT NOON.

'What d'ya think it means?' asked Nesbitt.

'I don't know,' said Laing quietly.

'What's a rubicon and how do you

get across one?' Nesbitt persisted.

'I don't know,' said Laing again, 'but I got a feelin' I need to find out quick. Thanks for all your help.'

Laing shook Nesbitt's hand warmly and headed for the door, then stopped.

'Say, when was this message delivered to this Major Kramer?'

'Hey. That's a good question. I've been here since seven thirty this morning and I didn't even know we'd received the telegraph until you spoke about it.'

'It was sent just after midnight last night so someone must have picked it up.'

Nesbitt scratched his head.

'They couldn't have. I closed our office at six o'clock last night and opened it again this morning.'

'You have someone else who works here could work a telegraph?'

'Well there's only Barney Cartwright. He's my sort of under-manager, but . . . '

Suddenly, a deep frown spread across Nesbitt's face. 'He wouldn't have . . .

hang on a minute, Mr Laing.'

Nesbitt went to the back of the office and shouted at the top of his voice.

'Barney? Barney? Get your skinny hide out here, will ya?'

Barney Cartwright was a thin, sullen boy with bad skin who shuffled when he walked. He was about twenty, though with his rounded back and the way he stared at the floor when he talked, he looked like an old man.

'Got something to ask you,' said Nesbitt sternly.

'Who's he?' asked Cartwright sullenly, glaring at Laing.

'He's a Pinkerton agent in a mighty hurry!' Nesbitt slapped his hand over his mouth and looked at Laing in alarm. 'Sorry! I wasn't meant to say who you were, was I?'

'That's all right. In this case, I think it's better our young friend knows who I am and what I can do to him if he starts tellin' me lies.'

Cartwright suddenly looked up and his mouth slipped open, showing two rows of rotten teeth.

'Ask him anything, Mr Laing,' said Nesbitt.

'You know how to use this telegraph?'

'Yes.'

'You received any messages for a Major Kramer recently?'

'I . . . I . . . don't know what you're talking about.'

'Listen, son. Don't make it harder on yourself. You're in enough trouble as it is,' said Laing. 'Did you come in here last night and pick up a message for Major Kramer?'

Cartwright looked at Nesbitt then stared at the floor.

'Yes, I did.'

Nesbitt took a step forward with his hand raised. 'Why, you little — '

'Wait! You can deal with him later. I just need to know a couple of things and then I'll be on my way.'

Nesbitt lowered his hand but continued to glare at the office boy.

'So, what did they promise you?'

'They gave me fifty dollars if I would come in here when Mr Nesbitt was gone and pick up any messages that came for a Major Kramer and then I had to take them to him over at Ruby's.'

'Fifty dollars!' exclaimed Nesbitt. Laing held up his hand.

'How long has this been going on?'

'A few weeks.'

'How many messages?'

''Bout a dozen or so.'

'What did they say?'

'I couldn't make no sense of any of them.'

'You don't remember any of them?'

'No. I wasn't payin' that much attention. If they wanted to pay me all that money for sendin' a lot of tomfoolery through the wire, then that was up to them.'

'You don't remember anything about them?'

The boy thought for a moment then said, 'I remember they used the word rubicon a lot.'

'You know what that means?'

'Ain't got a clue!'

'OK.' Laing turned to Nesbitt. 'That's all I need. I gotta go.'

'What'll I do with him?' asked Nesbitt, nodding at the boy.

'Do what you like. One last thing, boy.'

'Yes?'

'This Major Kramer. What does he look like? Can you describe him?'

Cartwright looked over Laing's shoulder.

'Don't need to. Turn around and see him for yourself. That's him crossing the street now.'

11

Kramer and Ethan made their way through the crowd which was slowly drifting towards the station. Word had spread that the senator was to speak at noon. They crossed the street and stepped up onto the sidewalk outside a boarded-up store. The weather-beaten sign above the door read, Abraham Wiseman. Tailor and Gentleman's Outfitters.

'In here,' murmered Kramer. He looked around him as he took a large brass key from his coat pocket.

'Who owns this place?' asked Ethan.

'We do,' said Kramer.

The key turned easily in the lock but he had to push hard against the warped timber door to open it. He signalled Ethan to enter the store, then followed him in.

As Kramer locked the door behind

them, Ethan looked around. A few empty crates lay discarded on the dirty floor. There was a dust-covered counter with a wall of empty shelves behind it. The place smelled musty and Ethan reckoned it must have been lying empty for a while. It was dark. Just a few shafts of sunlight slipped through the gaps in the boards on the windows.

'Follow me,' ordered Kramer.

The two men walked to the rear of the store where a narrow set of stairs rose steeply to the next floor. At the top of the stairs there was a landing with three doors leading off it. Kramer approached the first door on his left and, taking out another brass key, unlocked it and pushed it open.

The room was clean and tidy. Behind the door was a small table with a kerosene lamp in the centre and two chairs on either side of it. Against a wall was a cot with a blanket neatly spread on it as though someone was expecting to stay. Kramer strolled over to the window on the facing wall.

'Let me show you something,' he said, pointing out of the window.

Ethan walked over and immediately understood why Kramer had picked this place. There was a clear view of the bunting-clad platform. Over the heads of the gathering crowd, he could clearly see the lectern and rows of seats that had been laid out for the invited dignitaries.

'What'ya think?' grinned Kramer. 'When the senator gets up to say his few words, you'll have the best view in town. You got a clear shot. Can't miss.'

Ethan stared at him. 'Are you kiddin' me? It's gotta be at least nine hundred yards.'

'Nine hundred and twenty-eight, to be accurate.'

'I ain't that good. It can't be done.'

Kramer put his hand on Ethan's shoulder and squeezed it.

'I know how good you are, boy. You forget I've seen you in action that day up on Chinn Ridge.'

'But . . . '

Major Kramer held his finger up to silence Ethan.

'You think we ain't thought this through? We ain't gonna ask you to do a job and then not give you the tools to do it with.'

He walked over to the cot and pulled back the blanket. Lying on the mattress was a slim wooden box. He carried it over to the table, undid two clips on the front and pushed the lid back.

'Come and have a look at this,' he said.

Lying in the satin-lined box was a rifle that Ethan instantly recognized.

'It's a Whitworth. One of the few we managed to hide at the end of the war.'

Kramer opened a compartment beside the rifle and took out a cardboard box. He removed the lid and lifted out a cartridge, turning it between his thumb and fore-finger.

'This is the last of the ammo too. Only got a few dozen left; but that's not a problem. You only need one.'

He peeled back a section of the linen

cloth and below it was a slim, black tube.

'Improved sight. Five times magnification. It'll be like you were standing next to the man.'

While Ethan stared at the deadly weapon, Kramer knelt down and reached under the cot. He pulled out what looked like a number of black tent poles.

'This here's the tripod. We'll set it up over at the window. The window's been altered so all you do is loosen two bolts and the window frame swings out.'

Kramer placed the tripod in front of the window, attached the gun and peered through the telescope.

'Now you got everything you need: you got a clear shot; you got the gun, the bullet and the sight. And you got the motivation. You just need to pull the trigger.'

'If it's that easy, then why don't you do this yourself?' asked Ethan.

Kramer smiled. 'You know it's not as simple as that. Still takes skill. Still takes a steady hand. Besides, I've got other things to attend to while you're up here. Go ahead, see how it feels.'

Ethan walked to the gun. He had to admit, it was a beautiful, deadly thing. He put his hands around the stock and barrel and nestled it into his shoulder.

'She's lovely, ain't she?' beamed Kramer. 'She'll do the job, all right.'

Ethan looked through the telescope. The crowd filled the lens. He lined up the cross hairs on the side of the head of one of the men in the crowd. And suddenly he was back up on Chinn Ridge. He felt sweat starting to break on his brow. He closed his eyes tightly.

'What's wrong, boy?'

'Major Kramer. I'm askin' you one last time. Don't make me do this.'

Kramer was suddenly angry.

'What is the matter with you, boy? You want your child to die? Is that what you want, Corporal?'

Suddenly, Ethan felt a bitter rage well in his chest. He was tired of being pushed around, being told what to do, and being used as a pawn in these people's sick political games. Ethan lunged at Kramer and grabbed him by the lapels of his coat. His hat fell to the floor as Ethan banged him hard against the wall.

'If you so much as lay one finger on Lucy, so help me, I will kill you, Kramer!' screamed Ethan.

Kramer smiled.

'That's good,' he said quietly. 'So you ain't completely yella. There's some fightin' spirit in you after all. You wanna kill me? Go ahead. But if I don't check in with Finnegan every fifteen minutes, he puts a slug through her head. You decide.'

Ethan tightened his grip across Kramer's lapels, pressing hard against his neck, slowly closing off his air supply.

'It's just one shot,' gasped Kramer.

'And what then? You just gonna let me go? And Lucy too? There's nothin' to stop you killin' both of us once I've done your dirty work!'

'You have my word . . . as an officer . . . and a gentleman,' whispered Kramer.

'An officer and a gentleman?' shouted Ethan. 'You are a disgrace to this uniform and all the men who died wearing it.'

Kramer started to choke.

'You got five minutes before Finnegan starts wonderin' where I am . . . '

Ethan's grip grew tighter. He stared into Kramer's eyes and knew in another few minutes he would throttle the life out of him and not lose a wink of sleep over it. It would be so easy to do.

With a curse, he released his grip and stood back. He had no choice. He was trapped as long as they had Lucy.

Kramer leaned against the wall, gasping for air, pulling his tunic away from his throat. Then he pushed himself off the wall and leapt towards Ethan, his fist swung back. Ethan took the full force of the punch. He spun back and landed heavily on the cot.

Kramer stood over him, panting heavily.

'Don't you ever lay your filthy hands on me again, Corporal. Damn you. I've hanged men for less!'

Ethan clung to the side of the cot. He spat a wad of blood onto the floor.

'Now,' said Kramer, straightening his uniform, 'I suggest you pull yourself together and focus on the mission. Familiarize yourself with your weapon and I'll go see if I can stop Finnegan's itchy trigger finger. That man follows my orders to the letter. I suggest you start doing the same.'

Kramer walked to the door.

'And just in case you get any other crazy notions, we'll be watchin'. Y'hear me?'

Ethan stared at the floor.

'What was that, Corporal?' said Kramer, halfway out of the door.

'Yes, sir,' he mumbled.

'That's better,' said Kramer. He banged the door behind him. Ethan listened to Kramer's boots go down the stairs and cross the store below. When he was sure Kramer had left the building, he lay back on the cot and stared up at the ceiling.

There had to be a way out of this.

There just had to be!

12

Behind the bar in Ruby's saloon, there was a small room with a cooking range where Ruby sometimes fixed vittles for gamblers who didn't want to leave their hands. She was in there now, putting a plate of beans, biscuits and a pot of coffee on a tin tray. She then carefully carried it through the saloon and up the stairs to the landing. At Kramer's room, she took a deep breath to calm her churning nerves, then balanced the tray on her knee and tapped the door three times.

'Who is it?' boomed Finnegan's voice.

'It's Ruby. Kramer told me to bring you some food.'

'Wait a minute.'

Ruby put her head close to the door and heard Finnegan's heavy footfall as he crossed the room. But she heard something else, too. Lighter steps and a soft, muffled voice which Finnegan responded to in an urgent whisper.

When she heard Finnegan approach the door, she stood back. The lock turned. The door opened a few inches and Finnegan's face appeared in the crack.

'You alone?' he asked.

'No, I brought the cavalry with me — of course I'm alone!' said Ruby, sounding a lot braver than she felt.

Finnegan chortled and stepped back to let Ruby into the room. She looked around quickly. Everything looked just as it was when she had rented the room out to Kramer except she noticed the key to the side-room door was missing.

'Sure smells good,' said Finnegan, sniffing over the tray appreciatively.

'I'll set your things out on the table.'

'No need. I'll be fine.'

He went to take the tray from her but she swept past him.

'It's no bother,' insisted Ruby as she started to lay out his cutlery on the small table by the window. 'What you doin' all cooped up here on your own, anyway?'

'Just followin' orders,' said Finnegan.

Ruby pulled a chair from the table.

'Come on and sit down. I'll stay with you a little while, if you like.'

Finnegan's eye narrowed in suspicion.

'What fer?'

'We could have a little chat. Pass the time of day. Don't you get lonesome, Sergeant? I know I do.'

Finnegan looked Ruby up and down and smiled widely, rubbing his beard.

'Somethin' I gotta do first.'

'What's that, Sergeant?'

'I gotta . . . you know . . . go to the . . . '

'Oh, sure. You go ahead. I'll be here when you get back.'

Finnegan glanced at the adjoining room. He seemed torn between leaving Ruby alone in the room and not wanting her to go. He made up his mind.

'OK. You just sit tight. I'll be back in five minutes.'

Ruby smiled as Finnegan left the room. She didn't move until she heard him reach the bottom of the stairs, then she quickly crossed the room and knelt down at the lock of the side door. She was beginning to think that maybe the other voice had been her imagination. She turned the handle on the door and pushed against it. As she guessed, it was locked. She felt under her apron and brought out a ring of keys. Her fingers were trembling as she found the right key and slipped it into the lock. As she turned it, she paused to listen for any sound on the stairs and then, with a deep breath, went into the room.

It was dark. The heavy drapes had been drawn tightly and it took a few moments for her eyes to adjust to the gloom. When they did, she caught her breath in shock. Sitting on a chair in the corner, a small girl stared back at her.

As Ruby walked to her, she realized

the little girl's hands had been bound to the chair and a blue bandanna was tied tightly around her mouth.

'It's OK, honey. I ain't gonna hurt you,' whispered Ruby.

The little girl sat still, her eyes wide, not daring to move. Ruby saw dark tearstains down her cheeks. She was frightened but otherwise she looked unharmed.

'Oh, my dear Lord!' murmured Ruby, as she kneeled down in front of her. Ruby put her finger to her lips firmly to say that she could not make a noise, then carefully she loosened the gag behind her head and pulled it away. The little girl let out a gasp of air.

'For pity's sake, child, who are you?'

The girl took a deep breath. 'My name is Lucy van Kirk.'

'You OK, Lucy? You hurt?'

Lucy shook her head.

'Is your pa called Ethan?' asked Ruby.

'Yes! You know him?'

'I've met him. He told me you might

be here. I . . . I didn't believe him.'

'You seen that giant man with the patch? Him and some other men. They want my pa to do a real bad thing and if he doesn't do it, they say they're gonna kill me.' As she spoke the tears started to roll down her face. 'I want my pa!'

Ruby pulled Lucy's head to her chest and hugged her tightly.

'Nobody's gonna hurt you. You understand?' she said fiercely. 'I promise you. I'll get you outa this and we'll go find your pa together.'

She started to untie the girl's hands, then stopped. There was a noise on the stairs! If Finnegan found her in here, chances were he would kill them both. She took Lucy's head in her hands and spoke in quiet, urgent whispers.

'Lucy! Lucy! Listen to me! I promise you I'm gonna get you outa this but you gotta stay here just a little bit longer.'

The child started to sob again.

'I know you don't want to and it

breaks my heart to leave you but I promise you, I promise you with the last breath in my body, I will come back for you. I just gotta think of a way of doing it without gettin' us all killed. You understand?'

Lucy nodded, and sniffed loudly.

'Good girl! Now I gotta put this back around your mouth and you cannot tell anyone you talked to me. OK?'

'Wait!'

'What is it, baby?'

'See this locket round my neck?'

'Yeah.'

'Take it and give it to my pa. He'll know I'm safe.'

'Lucy, I — '

'Please?'

As Ruby reached around to undo the clasp at the back of the girl's neck, she could hear Finnegan whistling softly as he lumbered up the stairs. She slipped the locket into the front pocket of her apron.

'What's your name?' Lucy whispered.

'Ruby.'

'Ruby,' repeated Lucy. 'Did Ma send you?'

'Yes, darlin'. Your ma sent me.'

Ruby bit her bottom lip as she pulled the gag back up around Lucy's mouth again and gently stroked her long dark hair.

'I'll be back for you, I promise,' she whispered, then tiptoed quickly across the room, grimacing at every squeak of the floorboards.

She slipped into the bedroom and as she fumbled with the key in the lock, she watched in horror as the door started to open. She flipped the key over, slipped the key ring below her petticoat and quickly pulled out a cloth from one of her apron pockets and started hastily dusting a painting hanging near the door.

Finnegan stopped in the doorway.

'What you doin' over there, Ruby?'

Ruby smiled. 'Saw some dust on this picture. Thought I would just keep the place spick and span for you.'

'It's fine. Leave it. You can clean up

when we've moved on.'

'And when would that be?' asked Ruby innocently.

'Tonight. Once the senator's gone. Then we'll be on our way.'

'Gone?' said Ruby. 'What do you mean, gone?'

'Well, when he's finished his speech and he's back on the train headin' to his next rally. What did you think I meant?'

'Oh, nothin',' said Ruby.

Finnegan looked across at the table where his meal was set out. 'You joining me?'

'I know I said I would stay, but I've just remembered I got something I need to attend to. I'll call by later.'

'Thought you said you wanted to spend some time with me?' said Finnegan, looking hurt.

'I do. I really do, but ... this is important.' She made her way to the door, aware that Finnegan was watching her closely with a perplexed look on his face. 'You need anything else, you be sure to just give me a call, y'hear?'

Finnegan nodded and then she slipped out into the corridor. As she stood outside, trying to stop her heart from pounding out of her chest, she heard Finnegan cross the room and for an awful moment, she thought the door would swing open and he would come out looking for her. But she heard the lock turn and Finnegan walk back over to the table by the window. She put the back of her hand to her forehead and let out a long, slow, shuddering breath.

So van Kirk had been telling the truth all along!

She reached into her apron pocket and lifted out the small gold locket. She stared at it nestling in the palm of her hand, then closed her fingers tightly over it. She didn't know how, but if it was the last thing she did, she was going to get that little girl away from Major Kramer and his men and deliver her safe to her pa.

13

Ethan lay on the cot for what seemed an eternity. His mind kept spinning, trying to get a grip on this nightmare in which he found himself.

All he had wanted was to spend a day with his daughter, to try to start and put everything behind him, a chance to try and be a normal family. After everything he had been through, was this too much to ask?

He sat up angrily. Feeling sorry for himself was not going to get Lucy back and that was what he had to focus on. It didn't matter if he came out of this or not. All that mattered was that Lucy did. He had to start *thinking*.

But every time he came up with a plan, he found a flaw in it. Kramer and Crane and whoever else was involved in this had had a lot of time to think all this through and it looked as though they had covered all the angles. They had all their people in place; people Ethan didn't even know about . . .

People . . .

That was the key. This was too big for him to tackle on his own. He needed someone on his side! Even one would tip the scales in his favour. There must be someone in Cotton Junction who could help?

And then it struck him! Daryl Winters, of course! Why hadn't he thought of it before? Hadn't he said he was helping to protect the senator and he had a small army to help him do it? Ethan felt a sudden surge of energy and relief flood through him.

He jumped up from the cot, went over to the window and peered through the telescopic sight. He swept the platform and sure enough, there was Daryl talking to one of his deputies.

He ran out of the room and leapt down the stairs two at a time. As he grabbed the handle of the door, he stopped and took a deep breath. He would have to be careful. Kramer had said he had men everywhere. Slowly, he pulled the door open and peered into the busy sidewalk.

A boy, about ten years old, ran past.

'Hey, sonny!' hissed Ethan. The boy skidded to a halt in front of him.

'Wanna earn a dollar?'

'A whole dollar?'

'Yessir. All to yourself.'

'Show me.'

Ethan went into the top of his waistcoat and pulled out the coin.

The young boy eyed him suspiciously. 'What've I gotta do?'

'I want you to go round to the station and find Sheriff Winters. Tell him Ethan van Kirk sent you. Tell him to meet me at Ruby's. I'll be standing at the bar. And listen, this is real important, tell him it's a matter of life and death. Y'hear me? Life and death. You got all that?'

Ethan made the boy repeat the message a couple of times to make sure he had it right.

'Can I trust you, son?'

'Sure you can, mister.'

Ethan gave him the dollar.

'OK. On you go as fast as you can and get the sheriff.'

Ethan watched as the boy sprinted down the sidewalk and disappeared around the corner. He closed the door and leaned against it. As he stood in the cool gloom of the store with his eyes closed, he said a small prayer that the boy would deliver his message. He waited for his heart to slow to somewhere normal, then he opened the door again and stepped out onto the boardwalk. He quickly looked around to see if he was being watched before he closed the door behind him and crossed the busy street to Ruby's.

When he reached the batwings, he stopped and looked over them. The bar was still busy but he couldn't see Kramer or Finnegan or Ruby. He pushed in and made his way to the bar and ordered a whiskey from the barkeep. He had barely put it to his lips when he felt someone brush his shoulder.

'A boy says it's mighty urgent you speak to me,' said Daryl quietly.

Ethan fought the urge to turn and shake him warmly by the hand. He stared at the bar as he put his drink down.

'Thank God you came, Daryl.'

'What in hell is this all about, Ethan?'

'Were you followed, do you think?'

The sheriff made to turn around and look behind him.

'Don't,' whispered Ethan, 'just keep looking forward.'

'Followed? I wasn't followed. You wanna start tellin' me what this is about?'

'They've got Lucy. They're gonna kill her if I don't kill the senator today at noon.'

'Whoa, whoa,' said Daryl. 'Who, exactly, has got Lucy?'

'There's a gang of them. An officer from my old unit. A crazy sonofabitch called Kramer. And a Sergeant Finnegan. But they got people everywhere.

They've even got someone close to the senator organizing things from the inside. A guy called Crane.'

Daryl said nothing. He stared at Ethan in the large mirror behind the bar.

'Don't look at me like that, Daryl,' said Ethan. 'You're the only chance I have left. You believe me, don't you?'

'I believe somethin's goin' on we need to get to the bottom of,' said Daryl quietly. 'You know where they've got Lucy?'

'Here. In a room upstairs.'

'Here?'

'Yep. Top of the stairs. First door on the left.'

'Ruby know about this?'

'I think she's in on it too. Suppose she's got to be, hasn't she?' Ethan downed the rest of the whiskey. 'Truth be told, I'm gettin' to the stage I don't know who I can trust.'

'OK.' Daryl pushed away from the bar. 'Let's go and sort this out. Follow me.'

'You gonna go youself? Ain't you gonna get some help?'

Daryl pointed to his badge. 'I think I got all the help I need.'

Ethan grabbed Daryl's arm.

'Thank God you're here, Daryl. I had nobody else to turn to.'

The sheriff smiled and laid a hand on Ethan's shoulder. 'We're friends, ain't we?'

Ethan nodded, then followed the sheriff towards the stairs. They went up together, making as little noise as they could. When they arrived at the top of the stairs, Daryl pointed to the door.

'This it?'

'Be careful, Daryl, remember they've got Lucy.'

Winters nodded then stepped towards the door. He stood to one side, listening for any movement behind it, and beckoned on Ethan to come and join him.

'What are you gonna do, Sheriff?' whispered Ethan.

'I'm gonna surprise 'em.'

He rapped three times on the door.

'Who's there?' came a muffled voice.

'Sheriff Winters. Open up!'

Ethan stood back, bracing himself for gunshots to come through the door, but instead he heard the door unlock. Finnegan's face appeared.

'Sheriff Winters. How can I help you?'

Daryl pushed on the door with the flat of his hand and Finnegan stepped back.

'Come on, Ethan,' said Daryl, stepping into the room.

Ethan couldn't believe it was going to be this easy. He stood behind Daryl. Kramer was at the window with his back to them. Finnegan guarded the door to the side room.

'Close the door, Ethan,' said Daryl. When he did, Kramer turned around and stared at the two men. Ethan stepped forward and pointed at him angrily.

'That's your man, Sheriff. That's the man who kidnapped my daughter and is gonna kill the senator and — '

As he was speaking, Kramer walked towards him. He didn't get to finish the sentence as Kramer's fist smashed into his gut. The room spun and his eyes misted over. He felt his legs give way beneath him and he crumpled to the floor. When he looked up, Kramer was standing over him.

'Corporal van Kirk. You are a major disappointment. Can't you take a direct order any more? I told you not to get any ideas, didn't I? Didn't I tell you we had people everywhere?'

Ethan rolled onto his back and looked up at Daryl. He was standing with his thumbs hooked in his gunbelt.

'Daryl . . . help me . . . ' gasped Ethan and then, with what felt like a thud to his brain, Ethan realized what was happening. 'You . . . you're in on this?' he whispered in disbelief.

'I'm sorry, Ethan. But when I saw you this morning, you were like a gift. The best sharpshooter I ever knew and you appear on the day we needed you.'

'You put them up to this?'

'It was all in place already. You were an unexpected bonus.'

Ethan shook his head. 'You said you were my friend . . . '

'It ain't personal, Ethan. It's just politics.'

Kramer walked back over to the window and stared out. 'That's enough, Sheriff. You can go now.'

'I'll see you later, Ethan,' said the sheriff as he walked to the door. 'Just do what the major asks you and everything'll be just fine.'

Ethan lay on the floor in a daze. In the distance, he heard Kramer's voice.

'Didn't I tell you? Didn't I tell you that you are on your own? You can't take us on. There is no way out of this other than to complete your mission. You try anything like that again and I will skin your little girl like a rabbit in front of your eyes. You got that, Corporal?'

Ethan nodded.

'Now time is a-wastin'. Get up!'

Ethan rolled onto his hands and

knees and then unsteadily raised himself to his feet. Kramer crossed the room and stood in front of him.

'Now, come on, boy. Pull yourself together. You get yourself across that road and you do what you're best at. That's all you have to do. Just follow my orders and soon this will be all over.'

Finnegan opened the door and, without a word or glance back, Ethan walked out of the room and down the stairs.

His last hope was gone.

He truly was alone in the world.

14

There was an uncomfortable silence in the railway car as Laing and Crane watched Senator Grimley try to button his starched collar. Even with his head stretched right back, he was finding it difficult to fasten the stud against the rolls of fat beneath his chin.

'Damn collar,' he mumbled under his breath, 'I'm sure they've packed the wrong size.'

Laing and Crane said nothing and waited patiently while the senator fixed the stud and tied a black cravat to his satisfaction. Eventually, panting slightly from his struggle, he flipped open his pocket watch and glanced at the time.

'So let me get this straight, Mr Laing. It is now half past eleven. With thirty minutes to go before I go out and address the good citizens of Cotton Junction, you are suggesting I cancel?

You're asking me to stay on this train and just pull out? Is that what you are saying?'

Laing nodded. 'In a nutshell, Senator, aye.'

The senator looked at the carpet and nodded slowly. 'And this preposterous proposal is based on what?'

'Some information has come to light.'

'What information?'

'I'd rather not disclose that right now.'

The senator sighed impatiently.

'Look, Mr Laing. I like to think I'm a reasonable man, but if you are seriously asking me to consider your suggestion, surely I need all the facts to hand?'

'I don't have all the facts, sir, I only ask that you trust my experience in these matters.'

'Mr Laing, much as I respect your judgement, I'm afraid that is not enough. I need more.'

Laing shifted uncomfortably. He glanced across at Crane. The smirk spread across his face said it all. Then he turned back to the senator.

'Very well, sir.' Laing took a deep breath. 'I have a feeling — '

'You have a *feeling?*' Grimley repeated incredulously. 'And based on that you want me to abandon my schedule and scuttle out of town like a frightened cur with its tail between its legs? Mr Laing, this is the nineteenth century. We are men of progress and science, not of portents and signs and . . . *feelings*. What do you make of it, Crane?'

'You know my opinion, sir. I was never convinced of the need for Mr Laing to accompany us. With all his talk of plots and conspiracies, I am beginning to believe that Mr Laing may have his own reasons for not having you make this speech.'

'That's not true! I have no other reason — '

'Really? You seem to be offended that I am accusing you of plotting against the senator when only last night, you accused me!'

'Is that right, sir?' asked the senator, stony-faced. 'Did you accuse Mr Crane of plotting against me?'

'I did not directly accuse Mr Crane of anything, I merely — '

The senator brought himself up to his full height and tugged fiercely at the bottom of his waistcoat.

'Enough, sir, enough! I deeply respect the work your agency has done with the United States Government and you come highly recommended but I think, quite frankly, Mr Laing, this mission is out of your depth. Politics is a messy business. It means doing things you don't always want to do; dealing with people you'd rather not. It requires subtlety and diplomacy, skills I fear you do not possess, in order for you to continue to be part of my retinue. I will not have you insulting the most loyal and dedicated member of my office; especially when it is based on nothing more than a *feeling*.'

'Senator,' said Laing quietly, 'there have been a number of occasions when my gut instincts have proven to be correct. Mr Pinkerton himself — '

'That may be so, young man. And it may be all you need in the shadowy world you inhabit, but in my world — the real world — I am a politician and I need *facts!*'

He walked over to a gilt-framed mirror and picked a speck of dust from his sleeve and smoothed his jacket.

'Now, if there is nothing more, I would like to proceed with the task that I came here to do, namely, address the waiting voters.'

'Yes, sir,' said Laing.

'And afterwards, we will all enjoy a leisurely dinner to which we have invited a number of local dignatories including the local sheriff and some Confederate Army veterans. I intend to make sure that my stay in Cotton Junction is remembered for all the right reasons, Laing. I will not be leaving on your say-so. The matter is ended. Now, Crane, can we get on with the day's itinerary?'

Crane, with a triumphant smile on his face, opened the carriage door and stood back to allow the senator to pass.

'Thank you, Crane.'

'My pleasure, sir. It is time to cross the Rubicon!'

'It is indeed, Crane, it is indeed. Well said, sir.'

Laing looked up sharply, but Crane did not see his intent stare.

The senator, followed by Crane and Laing at his back, walked onto the platform. The brass band struck up and a roar rose from the crowd. Henderson stood near the steps in his best uniform and saluted the senator as he passed.

The senator waved, acknowledging the crowd's adulation. Laing hung back and spoke to the conductor.

'Mr Henderson, I wonder if you could do me a favour.'

'Yes, sir, If I can.'

'Speak to the engineer. Tell him to keep the boiler well stoked in case we need to leave in a hurry.'

'But I thought the senator was

planning to — '

'Plans can change and if we need to leave quickly, we'll need the train ready.'

'If you think it necessary, I suppose it'll do no harm.'

'I do — oh, and Henderson,' said Laing, as the conductor turned to leave, 'nobody else has to know about this. Just keep it between you and me for now.'

'Yes, sir,' said Henderson and strode off to the head of the train.

Laing made his way across the platform as he saw Crane take his seat on the front row of chairs. As he watched the senator play to the crowd, he put his hand into his jacket pocket and pulled out the slip of paper on which the telegraph clerk had scribbled down the message that was sent last night by Crane.

We cross the Rubicon at noon.

Laing looked across the heads of the crowds and felt a tight ball of nerves in his stomach as he sat beside Crane.

'Mind if I join you?'

'Please. Be my guest.'

Laing crossed his legs and leaned towards Crane.

'So you got your way. Congratulations. You won.'

'Not I, Mr Laing. Democracy is the winner today.'

Laing gazed out across the sea of bobbing heads, any of which could belong to a killer. He almost had a grudging admiration for the way Crane had set this all up.

'You know, Crane, there's something I'd like to ask you.'

'Ask away.'

'That phrase you used, you know, when the senator left the carriage. Something about crossing something?'

'The Rubicon. Crossing the Rubicon. You are not familiar with this phrase?'

Laing smiled. 'I'm not as educated as yourself, Mr Crane.'

'It's just a figure of speech. It simply means being committed to a course of action. No going back.'

'I see. But what does it literally mean? Where did the phrase come from?'

Crane smiled sympathetically at Laing, like a school-master to a slow pupil.

'Very well. The Rubicon is a river which marked the boundary between Gaul and Italy. In Roman times, no general was allowed to enter Italy at the head of an army. They had to be disbanded. To do so was an act of treason, punishable by death. In 49 BC Julius Caesar led a legion over the Rubicon, deliberately flouting the law. Once he'd crossed it, there was no going back. Hence, crossing the Rubicon.'

'And what happened?'

'Well, it was an act of insurrection, of course. War was inevitable, Mr Laing. Inevitable. Rome was plunged back into another bloody civil war.'

Laing stared at Horace Crane and suddenly everything fell into place. He flipped open his watch.

It was twenty-five minutes to noon.

15

Ethan stood on the boardwalk outside the batwings of Ruby's saloon and listened to the cheering coming from the station. He shambled across the deserted street, up the steps on the opposite boardwalk and into the empty tailor's shop. As he closed the door behind him, he looked at the stairs leading up to the room above where the gun waited for him. He was back where he started.

There was no way out of this now. He was going to have to go through with it. He felt the same way now as he had when he had been in the army. Powerless. Like a pawn in someone else's game. Don't think. Follow orders. Kill or be killed. That was what it boiled down to in the end.

When he reached the small room, he sat down on the cot and put his head into his hands. After a few minutes, he raised his head and listened. The crowd were quiet now. The band had stopped playing. He walked over to the window and stared down the sight.

There were two rows of chairs on the stage and behind a podium, a man in a black suit was making a speech. It had started. He lifted out his watch. In just twenty-five minutes, it would be noon.

Next to the speaker stood a rotund, white-whiskered elderly gentleman whom Ethan took to be the senator.

It wouldn't be long now. Soon, the senator would stand up and deliver his speech and he would do what he had to do. Only then would Ethan find out if they intended to give Lucy back to him. It was a gamble he would have to take. There was no other way.

A knock at the door jolted him from his thoughts.

'Who is it?'

'It's Ruby — from the saloon.'

'Go away,' called Ethan. 'I'm busy.'

There was a silence, then the door opened and Ruby came in carrying a tray. She smiled at him weakly and was about to say something when they heard the noise of boots coming up the stairs. Kramer appeared at the door, smiling broadly.

'Got Ruby to bring some grub over. Best keep your strength up.'

'I ain't hungry,' said Ethan.

Kramer glanced at the gun. 'You'd best be thinkin' about getting ready.'

'We got time,' said Ethan quietly.

Ruby put the tray down on the table. 'Brought you some stew and bread and hot coffee.'

Ethan looked up at her. Why did he keep getting people so wrong? What had made him believe she was someone he might be able to trust? What a fool he'd been!

'Told you, I ain't hungry,' he said, pushing the tray away.

Ruby stood watching him. She twisted her hands in her apron and seemed on edge, but then, Kramer made everyone nervous.

'At least take the cover off.'

'I told you, I ain't hungry. Take it away.'

Ruby glanced at Kramer, then turned to Ethan. 'I really think you should eat something.'

Ethan ignored her.

'Just leave it there, Ruby,' said Kramer. 'Maybe he'll feel like it later on.'

'At least drink the coffee while it's hot,' said Ruby.

'C'mon, Ruby. Time you were going,' said Kramer.

Ruby stared at Ethan, reluctant to leave, as though she wanted to say something, then she changed her mind. She glanced down at the tray again, then turned and left.

Kramer walked over to the table and lifted off the cloth cover.

'Smells good, though, don't it? Shame to waste it. She's a good cook, is Ruby.'

'Glad there's something good about

her. Just what kind of a woman gets involved in stuff like this? The kidnapping of a child. The murder of an innocent man.'

'What?' laughed Kramer. 'You think Ruby is part of this?'

'Well, ain't she?'

'You think I would let a feeble-minded woman into what we're doin'? She don't know nothin'. She knows nothin' about your kid.'

'But, the gun,' said Ethan. 'She's seen me here with the gun overlooking the stage. What does she think I'm doin' here?'

Kramer started to laugh. 'That's the crazy thing. She thinks we're part of the senator's guard. That's why she was told to keep it all secret. She thinks you're here to protect the senator, not kill him. You think she would let us hole up at her place if she knew what we were really doin'?'

'So she's not — '

'I told ya. She knows nothin'! Anyway, don't go wastin' her cookin'. I gotta go. I'll be up front when the senator starts talkin'. Don't want to miss the big moment, do I?' smiled Kramer.

As he left the room, Ethan looked down at the tray on the table. He was a liar. He was hungry. He reached across, lifted the tin bowl of stew and sniffed. He struggled to remember when he had last eaten. He looked for a spoon and, as he did, he realized there was a folded note lying on the tray. It must have been under the bowl.

He put the plate down and opened the note, which was written in fine, feminine handwriting.

Dear Mr van Kirk,
I have spoken to your daughter; Lucy. Under the coffee pot, you will find proof of this. She is well and unharmed. I intend to rescue her and get her to safety.
I now know what Kramer wants you to do and I am sorry I did not believe you. Do what you must do

and I will do the best I can for
Lucy,
God bless you,
Ruby Allison

Ethan re-read the note a few times. At first he thought it was a trap, but now he realized the risk Ruby had taken to get the note to him. That was why she had looked so frightened. Kramer would have killed her had he known.

Ethan lifted the coffee pot and saw the gold locket and chain. He gently lifted it and wrapped it in his hand. Lucy was alive! He slipped the chain over his neck and put the locket inside his shirt, then folded the note and put it into his top pocket.

Suddenly, he felt ravenous and started to spoon the stew into his mouth. He had only needed one person on his side. It looked as though he had one.

16

Ruby seldom drank the liquor she sold but when she got back to the saloon, she went straight behind the bar and poured a large measure of whiskey and swallowed it in one gulp. She stared at the batwing doors, waiting anxiously for Kramer to arrive. She would know by the look in his eyes whether he had discovered the note and the chain.

She was frightened and furious in equal measure. He'd taken her for a fool, telling her all that stuff about protecting the senator and needing a safe place to hide up for a few days. If she had even suspected that they were going to use her saloon for kidnap and murder, she never would have agreed to it. But, of course, Kramer had known that.

But there was no point in raking over cold coals. What she needed now was a plan. She had to think how she was going to rescue that poor kid. Her first instinct had been to go to Sheriff Winters but she'd seen the sheriff go up to the room a few times. Could he be involved in this too? With a sinking feeling in the pit of her gut she was beginning to realize there was no one in Cotton Junction she could completely trust. She realized that the only person who was going to get Lucy out was herself. But before she could even start to think about how she was going to do that, Kramer walked into the bar.

She lifted a glass and started polishing it with a cloth. She felt her heart start to pound in her throat, but she forced a smile onto her face. Kramer looked round the saloon for a minute, then approached the bar.

'Everything OK, Major?'

'Why wouldn't it be?' he growled.

'Just asking. Your boy over the street seems pretty wound up.'

'Yeah, well, guess he's got a lot on his mind. It's a big responsibility protecting the senator. Lot a people around who wouldn't mind if something happened to him.'

Suddenly, the glass slipped out of Ruby's hand. As it smashed at her feet, she let out a small cry.

Kramer looked at her closely. 'You're a bit jumpy yourself.'

'I'm fine. Just clumsy.'

'You got something on your mind you wanna talk about?'

'Me? Naw. I'm fine.'

Kramer nodded. 'OK, then. I'm going to check a few things, then head over to the station to catch the senator speaking. Wanna come with me?'

'Got a bit of cleanin' up here to do. You go ahead.'

'OK.' Kramer turned and headed out of the saloon.

Ruby felt the blood drain from her and she held the bar to steady herself. When she was sure Kramer was clear of the saloon, she took off her apron and threw it on the bar.

'Look after things, Walter,' she called

to the bar keep.

She walked to the stairs but at the bottom step, she hesitated. She had no idea of what she was going to do when she got to the top. All she knew was she had to get Finnegan out of the room long enough for her to get Lucy away from him. She knew if she got this wrong she would get herself and the kid killed. Maybe she should just let Ethan do the job and see what happened.

She had no idea what Kramer might do after Ethan had completed his side of the deal but she doubted he would even consider letting the girl go.

She placed a foot on the first step of the staircase and felt emboldened. She took another step and before she knew it, she was standing outside the door. Her hand was trembling as she raised it and knocked three times on the door. It opened slightly and Finnegan looked out.

'What's up, Ruby?'

'Nothing,' she said, smiling. 'Just came up to clear your things away.'

'Oh, sure. Come in.'

Finnegan let her in. The room was untidy with a newspaper scattered on the bed and empty coffee cups on the table. Ruby started to fuss around, gathering things up on to the tray. Finnegan locked the door and then went to sit by the window. He leaned back, stretching his legs out and putting his hands behind his head. Even with her back to him, she could feel his eyes wandering over her body and she did her best not to shudder with disgust.

'Heard your man bought it at Shiloh,' said Finnegan eventually.

'You heard right,' said Ruby, without turning round.

'Hell of a fight that was.'

'So I heard.'

'So you're on your own now. You're too young and pretty to be a widow,' said Finnegan, his voice low and threatening.

Ruby's instinct was to spin around and tell him it was none of his damn business, but she had to play for time to get him out of the way while she got Lucy away.

'That's nice of you to say, Sergeant.'

'You should get yourself a new man. Life's too short.'

Ruby turned around and looked at Finnegan. He was revolting. His belly sagged over his gunbelt and his ginger whiskers were overgrown and unkempt. His breath stank of tobacco and his hands and fingernails were filthy.

'Maybe I just ain't found the right man,' she said, as coquettishly as she could.

Finnegan smiled widely at her. 'And what sort of a man might you be lookin' fur?'

'Oh, I don't know. Someone tall. Handsome. Someone strong.'

Finnegan stood up and crossed to her, so close she could smell his foul breath. 'I think I know someone who fits the bill,' he said.

'You do?'

'Yes, ma'am.'

'And where might I find such a

gentleman, do you think?' she said.

'Oh, I don't think you'd have to go very far. Not far at all.'

He put his hands, as big as shovels, on her shoulders and made to move his face towards hers but Ruby put both hands on the giant's chest and arched her back away.

'Now, wait a minute, Sergeant. I think I know what we should do.'

'What?'

'Why don't you go down and see Walter behind the bar. Tell him I told you to get a bottle of our best whiskey. Then you can bring up two glasses and we can get cosy and you can tell me all about this gentleman.'

Finnegan smiled and rubbed his chin thoughtfully. 'Sounds mighty temptin', but I can't leave my post.'

'You'll only be gone a few minutes and I can keep an eye on things.'

'I don't know . . . '

Ruby stroked his arm.

'I would be very grateful if you could do this for me. *Very* grateful.'

A wide grin spread over Finnegan's face. 'Well, then, it would be ungentlemanly not to do what a lady asks,' he said.

'It would indeed,' smiled Ruby. 'I'll just make myself comfortable and wait here until you get back.'

'Yes, ma'am,' said Finnegan and wheeled around. Ruby heard his feet on the stairs as he pounded down them. She knew she didn't have long. She hurriedly pulled out her bunch of keys and, after a frantic search, found the key to let herself into the room.

As soon as she opened the door, Lucy sat up, her eyes wide in surprise.

'Come on, honey, we're gettin' you outa here,' said Ruby, as she pulled the gag from her mouth and started to untie the ropes looped around her wrists.

'You came back,' Lucy gasped.

'I told you I would, didn't I?'

Ruby cursed the ropes that refused to come undone, wasting valuable seconds. She could have kicked herself for not bringing a knife with her but eventually, they loosened and then fell away from around Lucy's wrists.

'Come on, honey. We gotta hurry. That big galoot could be back anytime.'

She grabbed Lucy's wrist and pulled her into the main room, then stopped. Finnegan was standing glowering at her with a bottle of whiskey in his hand.

'What in hell's name is goin' on here?'

Ruby pushed Lucy behind her.

'Don't you dare touch her,' she threatened.

Finnegan kicked the door with his heel. It shut with a bang.

'I think you should be more concerned about yourself, Miss Ruby. Wait 'til the major hears about this. He's gonna be real sore.' He took a step towards her. 'But first, I reckon I got a promise comin' my way. Once I get this little brat hog-tied again, you and me are gonna spend some time together. You think you can make a fool of me with all that pretty talk? C'm here, little girlie . . . '

Finnegan reached out to grab Lucy just as Ruby lashed out with her hand. Her nails scored down Finnegan's face, leaving a row of red welts. Finnegan howled and clutched his cheek.

'Why, you little wildcat! You're gonna be sorry you did that!'

He lunged forward. Ruby lashed out again but this time he caught her by the wrist and spun her around, wrapping both arms around her waist and lifting her off the ground.

She punched and kicked him as she struggled.

'Run, Lucy, run!' she screamed, Lucy dived for the door. As Finnegan tried to grab her he let Ruby go, dropping her to the floor. Ruby swiped her nails at his face again but Finnegan lashed out with a fist that caught her on the side of the face. She fell against the table, scattering the coffee pot and cups and saucers to the floor. Dazed but furious, she grabbed at the heavy coffee pot and lifted herself to her feet. Finnegan was approaching Lucy, who was pulling at the door handle, trying to get the door open. Ruby leapt across the room and brought the coffee pot down as hard as she could on the back of his head. He let out a cry like a wounded beast and wheeled round. A blind fury filled him as he reached behind his head and then looked at the blood on his fingertips. He took a few steps towards Ruby. Ruby backed away but then noticed that Lucy, behind his back, had dropped to her hands and knees and was hunched up behind Finnegan's legs. In a second, Ruby knew what she planned.

With a loud scream she lunged forward at the hulking giant, threw her full weight against him and shoved his chest. He staggered backwards and then stumbled against the girl crouched behind him.

Like a large redwood, he started to lose his balance. Arms swinging like a windmill, he fell backwards and landed with a sickening thud as his skull cracked on the floor. He passed out.

Lucy jumped to her feet.

'We did it! We did it, Ruby!'

Panting heavily, Ruby grabbed her by the hand. 'We ain't got time to celebrate, darlin', we gotta get to your pa!'

She grabbed the door handle and swung it open. Kramer filled the doorway.

'Well, hello, Ruby,' he said quietly. 'I was just coming to get Lucy here but looks like you saved me the trouble.'

17

Ethan unfastened the bolts that held the window into the frame. As it swung out, he took its weight, lifted it from its hinges and leaned it against the wall. He was glad of the soft breeze that blew into the room as he looked skywards and felt the heat of the noonday sun on his face.

A wave of applause and cheering suddenly rose up from the crowd and Ethan saw that the speaker at the lectern had finished and had turned to the stout, grey-haired gentleman on his right.

So, thought Ethan, this is the man I'm gonna kill today.

It was five minutes to noon. He turned back into the bedroom and moved the tripod to the window until the end of the barrel was in line with the ledge. Taking a deep breath, he took his place behind the gun and rubbed his palms. Beads of sweat were gathering on his brow and his mouth was dry. But he was surprised to find he felt calm. He held out his hands, palms down, and fanned his fingers. They were rock steady. His head was clear and he knew, for Lucy's sake, what he had to do.

He nestled the stock into his shoulder and curled his finger around the trigger. Adjusting his head slightly so his eyelashes were clear of the lens, he placed his eye to the telescopic sight. The stage came into view. Tilting the gun slightly, he adjusted the focus until he could clearly see everyone on the stage.

Standing behind the lectern, adjusting his collar in the midday heat, Senator Grimley was waving and smiling across the cheering crowd, oblivious of the imminent danger he was in. Ethan wondered what he would have done if he had known that at that very moment a gun was pointed at his head? Would he be frightened? This was a man who had not hesitated to send thousands of men to their deaths from the safety of an office in Washington. Ethan despised him and his kind, not enough to gun him down in cold blood, but if that was the only way he could get Lucy back, then Grimley's life was a price that would have to be paid.

Ethan moved the sight a little to the left. Horace Crane sat next to the senator, but Ethan could see his attention was elsewhere. There was a fine bead of sweat along his top lip which he dabbed nervously with a white linen handkerchief.

Ethan moved the sight again to take a look at the man sitting next to Crane. He didn't recognize him. His dusty bowler hat and crumpled brown suit looked out of place next to Crane's dapper suit and polished shoes. He had deep-brown, intelligent eyes which were bright and alive as he scanned the crowd, looking for something.

Ethan moved the gun and Daryl

Winter's face swung into view. He still couldn't believe this was someone he had once called 'friend'. He had stood at Ethan's side as he had buried Helen. Once, Ethan had told Lucy, if she was ever in trouble, Daryl was the man to go to. Now Daryl Winters had not just betrayed Ethan and his family, he was betraying his country, tarnishing the badge he wore with his treachery. Ethan felt his anger pulse through him. Ethan gripped the rifle so tight, his hands hurt. It would be so easy to squeeze this trigger. If there was one man who deserved to die this day, it was Daryl Winters. But he was not part of the Devil's deal.

In the sight, Ethan saw Daryl look to the right, looking for someone in the crowd. Ethan swung the sight, following his gaze. At the edge of the crowd stood Kramer. Ethan moved the sight up and down and, with a sharp intake of breath, realized that Lucy was standing in front of Kramer. He had his hands on her shoulders. She stood with her head bowed. Her cheeks were tearstained but she didn't look hurt. Ethan felt a wave of fury sweep through him. He pressed his eye firmly against the scope and adjusted it so that the cross hairs were placed squarely over Kramer's right eye.

'I oughta blow your head right off, you bastard,' murmered Ethan as he felt his finger start to tighten on the trigger.

Almost as if he had heard him, Kramer turned and looked straight in Ethan's direction. There was a smirk on his face and Ethan cursed him, knowing that killing Kramer would solve nothing. If anything happened to Kramer, Lucy would be killed immediately.

And, sure enough, even as Ethan thought this, Kramer leaned sideways to talk to someone. Beside him stood Finnegan and Ruby. She too was tearstained and her hair was dishevelled. Ethan could make out a livid bruise on the side of her cheek and he guessed what had happened. True to her word, she had tried to get to Lucy but had failed. Ethan felt his heart sink with despair but at the same time, felt a glow of gratitude. She had been his last hope and at least she had tried. She was the only one who had and he wondered if he would ever get the chance to thank her.

There was another roar of applause. Ethan swung the telescope back to the stage. At the lectern, the senator, with outspread hands, was urging the crowd to quieten down. A silence descended across the mob of faces and the senator smiled and began to speak.

'Ladies and gentlemen, girls and boys . . . '

Ethan lined up the cross hairs on his wide forehead and slowly started squeezing the trigger.

★   ★   ★

'He'd better make this quick,' muttered George Laing under his breath, as he watched the senator begin his speech.

He patted the outside of his jacket absent-mindedly and felt the reassuring bulge of his Colt Peacemaker with the shortened barrel that he wore in a shoulder holster under his right arm.

He glanced sideways at Horace Crane. He was unusually quiet. His foot tapped nervously and he kept patting his top lip with a linen handerchief. In the short time Laing had known him, it was the first time he had seen him like this. He felt sure it wasn't the rally. Crane would be used to events much larger than this. No, something else was going through his mind.

'Ladies and gentlemen, girls and boys,' boomed the senator. 'I am delighted to be here in Cotton Junction.'

As the senator moved into his well-rehearsed speech, Laing scanned the crowd. Standing up on the stage like this, in clear view of everyone, Grimley was a clear target.

Laing scanned the buildings across from the railway station. It was a long way, but a good shot might just be able to reach. He looked again at Crane, who was staring intently at someone in the crowd. Laing followed his gaze and saw a face he recognized. It was Kramer. Laing noticed he was holding a child and beside him was another soldier in uniform who looked as if he was holding on to a bedraggled woman.

In the warm sunshine among all these happy, cheering people, they stood out, looking tense and frightened. Laing knew there was something wrong.

Laing watched as the major lifted his hand and then raised three fingers. Crane nodded as if understanding the prearranged signal. Laing took out his watch and looked at it. It was three minutes to noon. Laing glanced at the major. He was pointing his finger towards the buildings across from the station. Crane was nodding again.

Laing stared at the buildings. Something was not right. He slowly raised his hand to his bowler and gently pulled the brim down to block out the glare of the high sun. The details of the buildings took shape as Laing narrowed his eyes to small slits.

Suddenly he realized what had been troubling him. It was not what was there, it was what was missing! Along the other buildings, people were hanging out of windows, waving flags, holding out banners. Children were being held aloft by their parents to get a better view.

But from one window there was nothing. No banner, no flag, nothing. As though this window was being kept for a special purpose. He was sure this was above the shop that Nesbitt said had been empty for months.

He felt a tight knot in the pit of his stomach as he looked across at Crane and then the major. They were both staring at the window too. Suddenly, he knew what he had to do.

' . . . and so, my message for you today, is that we must put our differences behind us. We are once more a united America and let nothing, nothing ever take us to the brink of terrible war again . . . '

Laing leapt out of his seat and sprang towards Grimley. A murmur, like a swarm of bees, spread through the crowd and somewhere a woman screamed as Laing's hand went inside his jacket and pulled out his gun.

Crane made to grab him but Laing pushed him away. The senator turned to see what the commotion was all about and, seeing Laing hurtle towards him, he raised his hands to protect himself. Laing dived on the senator, knocking him to the ground, then, placing himself in front of his body, he kneeled and fired three shots in quick succession above the heads of the crowd towards the window.

All hell broke loose. The crowd scattered like a herd of cattle in a thunderstorm. Women screamed, lifting children as they ran. Laing looked at the major. He was standing stock-still in among the pandemonium, staring back at him with a black hatred in his eyes.

Laing hauled the dazed senator to his feet.

'Senator! Senator! Can you hear me?'

'Uh? Yes . . . ?'

'We need to get on the train. Your life is at risk.'

Laing started to push the senator towards the train. He was just about to step onto the metal stairs when Laing saw Winters run towards him, his gun drawn. Laing pushed the senator behind him.

'Get out my way!' shouted Winters.

'You want to kill him, you'll need to go through me first!' said Laing.

'If that's the way you want it,' said Winters, raising his gun and cocking the hammer.

Laing saw his finger tighten on the trigger. Then suddenly a shot rang out. Laing winced and he heard the senator whimper behind his back. He looked at the sheriff. The gun was still in his hand but there was a strange, confused look on his face. Then slowly, he started to sink to his knees and, as he fell down, his head turned slightly and Laing realized half the side of his head was missing. It was splattered against the side of the railway carriage.

Laing spun and stared at the window. There was a curl of smoke rising from the window.

'Thank you — whoever you are,' he whispered under his breath. He was still staring when he heard footsteps run up behind him.

'Mr Laing! Mr Laing! Are you and the senator all right?'

'Yes, Mr Henderson. For now, but we need to get the senator out of here!'

'Good God,' said the conductor, staring at Winters's lifeless body.

'Mr Henderson, we really need to go . . . now!'

'Of course, Mr Laing.'

He turned and blew three loud blasts on his whistle. The train whistle replied and a shudder ran through the train as the engineer engaged the engine.

'Mr Henderson, do you have a gun?'

'A shotgun. In the caboose.'

'Good. Go get that and then meet me in the stateroom. This thing is not over yet!'

'Right, but — '

'There's no time to explain. Trust me.'

'Right, Mr Laing. I do.'

As Henderson ran along the platform, Laing turned and grabbed the senator's arm.

'Come on, sir. We need to get you out of here!'

He pushed the politician up the stairs and, as he did, he looked round. Crane was nowhere to be seen.

He would deal with him later.

18

Kramer stood stockstill amid the chaos that broke out all around him. He had seen Winters gunned down and knew who had done it and he was now glaring at Laing as he bundled the senator onto the train. But he did nothing. His army days had taught him that sometimes you had to react and sometimes it was better to wait to see how the cards fell.

Beside him, Lucy began to struggle. He tightened his grip on her wrist until she winced.

'Not so fast, little girlie. I still may need you.'

Kramer looked up at the window where Ethan should have been. He knew he could be seen clearly by the telescopic sight, but he also knew Ethan would never take the chance of taking a shot and risk hitting his child. The train's whistle shattered his thoughts and he realized Crane was standing in front of him.

'What'll we do now, Kramer?' he screamed. 'So much for your grand schemes! I knew you shouldn't have used that no-good sonofabitch!'

'It's not over yet,' said Kramer quietly.

'Not over? Not over? Winters is dead. The senator's escaped. Our plans are in tatters — and all because of you!'

'Get a grip of yourself!' hissed Kramer. Then he swung Lucy towards Crane. 'Take her with you and get on the train while you still can. Take one of Winters's men to deal with Laing. It's not over 'til I say it is, y'hear me?'

He pushed Lucy towards Crane, who grabbed her wrist.

'Where are you going?'

Kramer looked up to the window.

'Me and Mr van Kirk are goin' to have a chat.'

The train whistled again.

'You'd better go, Crane. You gotta train to catch.'

Crane cursed under his breath, then ran up the stairs and across the platform, dragging Lucy roughly behind him. Kramer saw him speak to a deputy then get on the train just as it started to pull away. He turned to Finnegan.

'Take care of Ruby,' he ordered, then disappeared into the crowd.

Finnegan grabbed Ruby's arm. 'Come on, little lady,' he grinned, 'we got some unfinished business to attend to.'

'Lucy! Lucy!' screamed Ruby, as she watched her board the train.

Finnegan laughed. 'No point in screaming. She's gone. Anyway, you're gonna need all the breath you got for what I got planned for you.'

He spun her around and put his arm across her neck. Ruby gasped for breath, but, as she thought of Lucy, a fierce surge of fury swept through her. She suddenly grabbed Finnegan's forearm with both hands and bit hard. She felt her teeth sink through his shirt, through skin and felt the tips of her teeth touch bone. Finnegan let out an animal roar and leapt back, clutching his arm in agony. Ruby stumbled forward but quickly gained her balance, swung round and brought her knee thumping into the giant's crotch. Finnegan groaned and, as he keeled over onto his knees in agony, Ruby lifted the hem of her dress and ran to the platform.

Finnegan rose to his feet and gave chase. Ruby ran towards the train, hoping to be able to jump on before the train picked up any more speed.

As the second-last carriage drew level with her, she prepared to jump. Then, just as she put out her hand to try and catch the handrail, she felt Finnegan's arms coil around her again.

'Why, you little slut. I'm going to make you pay for that!' he roared.

He spun her around and back-handed her across her cheek. The pain of it almost made her pass out and as she felt herself go weak at the knees,

Finnegan grabbed her around the waist with both arms and lifted her off the ground. He started to squeeze every ounce of breath out of her. Ruby began to feel dizzy and didn't know how long she could stay conscious. She was sure she could feel her ribs starting to crack and there was a dull roar rising in her head.

Finnegan was grinning wildly into her face. She could feel the awful warmth of his tobacco-tainted breath on her cheek. She knew she would not last much longer in the clutches of this animal. He was laughing, wide-eyed at her. One wide eye. Like a Cyclops! A one-eyed monster.

And suddenly, she knew what she had to do. She raised an arm behind her head and pulled out a long hairpin, which made her long dark hair fall around her shoulders. Out of the sun, her arm, came down in a powerful arc as she thrust the hair pin deep into his eye.

Finnegan let out an inhuman cry and

stepped backwards, clutching his eye and letting Ruby slip to the ground. As blood coursed down his face he spun wildly, trying to pull out the long wire pin. Ruby lay on the platform and watched the giant stagger. He twirled in a dance of agony, stepping closer to the edge of the platform as the train continued to pass. With the last of her strength, Ruby rose to her feet.

'Now die, you big sonofabitch,' she cried, as she ran at the giant, hitting him full in the belly. He wavered for a moment and then, just as the last carriage was level with him, his boots slipped over the edge of the platform and he slipped under the wheels of the train. If he screamed, his cry was lost in the plaintive sound of the whistle blowing as the train pulled out of Cotton Junction. Ruby stood gasping for air and watched the carriage slip from her grasp as it gathered speed.

With a wail of anguish, she fell to her knees, knowing she would never see Lucy again.

19

When George Laing had the senator on the train, he did not stop pushing him until they were down the corridor and in the safety of the stateroom. He helped the wheezing politician into a chair, then ran over to the window and looked out. With a grim smile of satisfaction, he saw they were pulling out of Cotton Junction, the train picking up speed with every passing minute. He pressed his face against the window and looked back down towards the town. The platform was deserted except for a weeping woman lying on the platform and he wondered for a moment if she had been hurt in the gunfire.

He turned to the senator. The old man was ash-white and was panting heavily, tugging at his collar as though he was having difficulty breathing.

'Are you all right, Senator?'

The senator managed to gather himself enough to reply. But if Laing was expecting gratitude for saving his life, he was very mistaken. The senator started wagging his finger angrily at him.

'I demand to know the meaning of this, young man. How dare you man-handle me like a . . . like a . . . common criminal? Rest assured Alan Pinkerton himself will hear of this and when he does — '

'Someone tried to kill you.'

'Kill me? Kill me? Bah. Preposterous! Crane was right. You think there are plots everywhere around you and — '

'You were about thirty seconds away from getting your head blown off.'

'By whom?'

'Ever since I have been on this train there has been a conspiracy against you, senator. A conspiracy of people very close to you.'

'What people? Why?'

Laing took a deep breath.

'Mr Crane for one. He was a part of a plot to assassinate you to start another war.'

The senator stared at the young man for a few moments, then he banged his hand on the arm of the chair and rose unsteadily to his feet.

'Enough! I insist you stop this! I will not hear a word said against Horace Crane. He has been a constant and loyal servant to me and yet you take every opportunity to besmirch his honour. I will not hear another word!'

At that moment, the carriage door opened and Horace Crane entered. Closing the door quietly behind him, he looked at both men in turn.

A wide smile of relief spread across the senator's face.

'Crane! Crane! How glad I am to see you, my boy. I want you to remove this man from my presence. The rally has been a disaster! We must get back to Cotton Junction at the earliest opportunity and — '

'Shut up!' said Crane.

The senator stopped as though he had been slapped in the face.

'I beg your pardon?'

'Shut up and sit down!'

'But . . . but . . . Crane, I don't understand.'

'Haven't you been listening to Mr Laing?'

'You mean . . . someone *was* trying to kill me?'

The senator sank slowly into his chair, shaking his head in disbelief. Crane slipped a hand in his pocket and, pulling out his derringer, turned to Laing.

'Please remove your weapon from your jacket, Mr Laing. Very slowly, if you please.'

Reluctantly, Laing reached inside his jacket and held the butt of the Peacemaker between his thumb and forefinger.

'Slide it along the floor towards me.'

'Crane,' whispered Grimley, 'what are you doing? Have you gone mad?'

'No, Senator, I'm not mad. I've never been clearer-headed in my life, despite

Mr Laing here trying to spoil my plans.'

'Your plans?' murmured the senator, turning to Laing.

'I went to the telegraph office and found the message Crane sent last night. I have it here. I knew you were up to something, but I didn't know what until you explained it yourself. When you told me what 'crossing the Rubicon' actually meant.'

Laing went into the inside pocket of his suit and pulled out the note. He passed it to the senator, who read it, then looked up.

'What is the meaning of this, Crane? I *demand* an explanation.'

'Don't! Don't demand!' shouted Crane, the gun trembling in his hand. 'You don't demand anything anymore from me, Senator.'

He turned to Laing.

'Happy with your little piece of detective work, Mr Laing? It didn't take too much to put it all together but I'm glad you have.' He looked at the senator.

'We've stood back and watched all of you bumbling fools in Washington make a mess of things for long enough. When Lincoln was assassinated — not before time — we had a high hope that the country would break apart, which is the way it should be. But all those sentimental fools, they felt so sorry for the man who almost wrecked our country.'

'He was a great man,' protested the senator.

'Let history be the judge of that.'

'You keep referring to *we*. Who is *we?*'

'There are a number of us. Strategically placed throughout government and the military. Just waiting for the right moment to rise and seize power.'

'Major Kramer's part of this, isn't he?' said Laing.

'Yes. He's looking forward to meeting you, Laing, after he takes care of another piece of business.'

'There must be more than just you and Kramer. Who was the assassin at the window?'

Crane's face clouded. 'He's a nobody. Totally dispensable.'

The senator rose to his feet unsteadily. 'Are you actually telling me that you and your compatriots are willing to plunge our glorious nation into war, with the death and destruction that we have already suffered? You would be willing to drive us down that bloody road again?'

'There are worse things than war, Senator. If that is what we need to do, then it must be done.'

'You do not use history as though it were your plaything, sir. You cannot manipulate events to your own ends,' said Grimley, angrily.

'Really? We'll see. Meanwhile, don't worry. You will have your footnote in the great events that are to be unleashed. Many great wars started with the death of a minor character. You are to play that role now, sir.'

With that, Crane lifted the derringer and pointed it at the senator's head.

'Goodbye, sir,' he said, as he started to squeeze the trigger.

20

Through the telescope, Ethan stared at his daughter standing on the footplate of the carriage and a wave of despair flowed through him. He had failed her.

And now she was being taken from him and he knew then deep in his heart that if that train disappeared around the bend and out of view, it would be the last time he would ever see his child. He was not going to let that happen!

Ethan calculated that he probably had about fifteen seconds, no more, until the train was either out of range or his shot was barred by outbuildings and trees.

He wiped his fingers on his chest. Sweat was rolling from his brow into his eyes and he blinked quickly to keep it away. He refocused his eyes down the lens. He could clearly see Lucy, standing in front of the deputy, a look of anguish on her face as she called out to Ruby still lying on the ground.

Ethan moved the sights to the deputy's chest along the row of shirt buttons, up to his neck and then to his chin, past his cold, blue, flinty eyes, and fixed on a spot right in the middle of his forehead but he couldn't keep it there. Every movement of the train spoiled his aim. It was an impossible shot. It was a million-to-one chance, but Kramer had said he could make the shot if he was motivated enough — he was motivated now!

Ethan took a deep breath to try and settle the pounding in his heart. He slowly, slowly started to increase the pressure on the trigger and gently squeezed.

The gun bucked in his arms but he controlled it tightly. The bang filled the room and he felt his nostrils flare with the acrid burn of gunpowder.

To Ethan, the world seemed to have slowed down. He was sure he had missed. Nothing happened. Nothing had changed: the train continued around the bend; Ruby lay on the platform; the deputy still held Lucy.

And then the deputy's head lolled backwards. A look of surprise spread across his face as a small bloom of red erupted in his forehead. His eyes were wide open as he slowly keeled over, his hands slipping from Lucy's shoulders as he crashed through the carriage doors behind him.

Even at this distance, Ethan heard Ruby screaming for Lucy. She had heard the shot and jumped to her feet and started running to catch up with the train like a mad woman.

'Jump, Lucy, jump!' she screamed.

Lucy had felt the deputy's hands release her and, although she did not know what had happened, she saw her chance and launched herself from the fast-moving train. As her feet touched the platform, she tripped and rolled like a piece of tumbleweed. She lay dazed, looking up at the blue sky, and the next thing she knew, Ruby was on her knees beside her, holding her tight in her arms.

Ethan watched all this happen and couldn't help but smile. At last, Lucy was safe. Ruby had her. He took his eye away from the eyepiece. It was over. He stepped away from the gun and walked over to the table and lifted his hat. All he had to do now was to go and collect Lucy and go home. It was all he had ever wanted to do. He turned to face the door just as it flew open.

Kramer stood in the doorway.

'You've been a big disappointment to me, Ethan,' he said, as he stepped into the room.

21

Crane raised the derringer at the senator, aimed it directly at his head and started to squeeze the trigger. The senator involuntarily closed his eyes and braced himself for the shot. Laing started to move towards Crane, knowing he would never close the distance between them before the bullet did its lethal work. But then Crane stopped as the carriage door behind them burst open. In a spray of shattered wood and broken glass, a lifeless body fell backwards into the carriage and with a muffled thud landed on the rug in the middle of the room. The three men stared at the deputy lying on his back, his eyes wide open, a stream of blood flowing across his face and onto the floor from a single, neat bullet hole in the centre of his forehead.

'Who on God's earth is this man?' cried Grimley.

Crane stared in silence at the dead man.

'He's one of the sheriff's men,' said Laing.

'The sheriff is in on this too?' gasped the senator in disbelief.

'Was,' said Laing.

Crane said nothing, transfixed by the corpse. It was the closest he had ever been to the reality of war.

'It's over, Crane,' said Laing quietly. 'Your plot's failed. There's nothing left.' He took a step forward and stretched out his hand. 'Give me the gun.'

Crane stared at him for a moment, a look of confusion on his face as though he could not grasp what was going on around him. He shook his head.

'No!' he cried, and pointed the gun again at the senator. 'Kramer's still out there. He'll pull things back. We can still do this thing. There *will* be a war!'

The gun cracked and leapt in his hand. The senator let out a cry and collapsed backwards into a plush chair, scrabbling at the front of his silk waistcoat, desperately trying to see where the bullet had entered.

Laing sprang across the room. Crane swung the gun in his direction and, with still a few paces between them, he fired the remaining barrel. But Laing did not falter. Grabbing the gun with his left hand, he brought his right fist up in a wide arc, crashing it onto Crane's jaw. Crane fell back like a stone, sprawling on the Persian rug. He stared up at Laing with a mixture of fear and disbelief.

'I've been waiting to do that for a long time. Get up!' ordered Laing.

Crane struggled to his feet but halfway up, he suddenly lunged towards Laing. He butted into his midriff and, as Laing groaned in agony, the two men fell in a heap on the floor beside the dead lawman. Crane started punching viciously at Laing's head, who did his best to deflect the blows, then he grabbed Crane's wrists and, pulling them apart, sat up quickly, head-butting Crane in the face. Crane fell back heavily, a mask of blood streaming from his nose and face.

'Give it up, Crane. It's over,' cried Laing.

Crane lay on his back, wiping the blood from his face. He looked at the back of his hand and the sight of his own blood seemed to enrage him. He looked around, desperately seeking a way of escape. He rose unsteadily to his feet.

He stood panting, staring at Laing with real venom in his eyes. He wiped the blood away again from his face.

'OK,' said Crane, panting heavily. 'You've won, Laing. This time. But there'll be a next time.'

Laing shook his head. 'There won't be a next time. You won't be able to do anything, locked up in the state penitentiary.'

'You'll have to catch me first, Detective.'

And with that, he turned and bounded out of the carriage. He was surprisingly nimble. With one foot on the rail between the carriages he leapt up, grabbed the top of the carriage and swung himself up onto the carriage roof. Laing leapt after him, but by the time he had raised himself up to look along the carriage, Crane was halfway along it.

'You're a damn fool, Crane. You can't get away!' shouted Laing.

Crane turned, his legs spread, steadying himself on the rocking carriage. He was laughing.

'Looks like this is my stop, Laing,' he said, getting ready to jump.

'Don't do it. I'll shoot.'

'No you won't,' laughed Crane. 'You're a man of honour. You wouldn't shoot an unarmed man.'

'No, but I would!' said a voice from the end of the carriage.

Crane turned to see Henderson, the conductor, with a shotgun pointed at him.

'Get off the roof, Mr Crane. You're under arrest.'

Crane moved closer to the edge of the roof and prepared to jump.

'I warned you!' shouted Henderson. The shotgun bucked in his arms. Crane stumbled, clutched his belly and, with a last glance back at Laing, toppled forwards with a scream and landed heavily at the side of the rails.

Laing watched the body shrink as the train left him behind. He raised his hand in salute to Henderson, then let himself slide down back onto the carriage floor and went into the railway carriage. The senator was where he had left him.

'You OK, Senator?'

The senator looked up dumbly. 'He . . . he . . . he shot me . . . ' he mumbled.

'Well, aye, he did, but you're not wounded.'

'I'm not?' asked the senator in disbelief.

'No, sir. Last night, when I followed Mr Crane, I noticed he carried a gun. I took the liberty of sneaking into his room and replacing his bullets with blanks, just in case things ever came to this.'

'You mean . . . ?'

'You're not wounded, sir.'

'Thank the Lord.' said the senator and slumped back into the plush chair with relief. Laing took his arm and helped sit him upright.

'I'll get you a brandy, sir. You've had a shock.'

'Thank you, thank you, Laing,' mumbled the old man as he sipped the reviving liquid.

'I never thought he *would* actually use it, though,' said Laing thoughtfully.

The senator looked at the deputy still lying on the floor, his blood beginning to dry and turn a dark brown.

'Was he the assassin? The man who tried to kill me up on the platform?' asked the old man.

'No. The shot was fired from a window from buildings directly across from the station. The shooter couldn't have fired the shot and then managed to get down from the building and get on board this train before it left the station. They just wouldn't have had the time.'

'Then my killer is still at large!' exclaimed the politician in alarm. 'He must be arrested at once. He must be stopped before he tries again!'

Laing shook his head slowly. 'There was a plot against your life, Senator. I'm not denying that. Whoever shot from that window was no amateur. I don't know the full story — we probably never will — but if the assassin had wanted you dead, you would be.'

'I don't understand. Are you saying he deliberately missed?'

Laing nodded. 'Aye. As strange as it may seem, that is what I'm saying.'

The senator shook his head in disbelief. 'But why?' he said eventually.

'I don't know. Who knows what deals men make with the Devil? We'll probably never know, but the one thing I do know for sure is that this guy had a job to do and for some reason he decided not to go through with it. He saved your life.'

'Maybe he just missed.'

'Men like him don't miss.' Laing looked down at the deputy's bloodied body, his head gently rocking from side to side with the movement of the train. 'And there's your proof right there.'

'What d'you mean?'

'This is what a real sharpshooter can do when he wants to. That must have been the best part of a thousand yards to a moving target with only one shot to make it count.'

Laing walked over to the window and looked out as Cotton Junction disappeared from view.

'He might be still out there and he sure is one hell of a shot, but he's no threat to you.'

The senator almost collapsed back in his chair and took another long swig of brandy. He rubbed his forehead with his fingers. 'This is almost too much to take in,' he muttered under his breath.

Laing walked across and put a hand on his shoulder.

'Why don't you go and rest for a while. Nothing else is going to happen here.'

'Yes, my boy, I think you're right. I think I will lie down for a moment.'

Laing helped the man to his unsteady feet. As the senator reached the door, he stopped.

'But what about this Major Kramer? Is he still a risk?'

'I don't think so. I got a feeling someone else will take care of him for us.'

The senator, not really understanding what Laing meant, just nodded.

'Mr Laing?'

'Yes?'

'I'm sorry I ever doubted you. Mr Crane had me believe — '

Laing held up his hand. 'You don't have to apologize, Senator. This is the job I was sent here to do.'

The senator smiled. 'Well, thank you, again.'

As the door quietly closed behind the senator, Laing walked over and sat down in the chair he had just left. He sat back and closed his eyes. He had promised himself he would not sleep until the senator was safe. With a tired groan, he let his head loll back. He would just close his eyes for a minute or two. He had earned that at least.

Within two minutes, George Laing, Pinkerton Detective Agent, despite his company's motto, was sound asleep and snoring gently.

22

'It's over, Kramer,' said Ethan.

'It may be over for you; it ain't over for us.' Kramer stepped into the room. 'You really tried to mess things up for us, didn't you, boy?'

'I told you. I never wanted any part in this. All I wanted was to go home with my little girl. That's what I still plan to do.'

Kramer shook his head. 'You think it ends here? You disobeyed my orders, Corporal. You didn't make the shot.'

'I made the shot OK. I just didn't hit the target you wanted me to.'

Kramer's mouth tightened in anger. 'Crane is with the senator. Finnegan's taken care of Ruby and we've still got your daughter. Seems to me things are still in place. Only one loose end to tie up.'

Ethan glanced out the window and

saw Ruby and Lucy were coming across the square, their arms wrapped around each other. He took a step towards the window and turned, blocking Kramer's view.

'And what might that loose end be, Major?'

'It's you, Corporal.' Kramer raised a pistol and pointed it directly at Ethan.

Without warning, Ethan suddenly lashed out at the rifle barrel. It spun on the tripod. Kramer instinctively ducked and, as he did, his gun went off but the slug buried itself harmlessly in the floorboards as the metal barrel came round and hit Kramer full on the side of his head.

Ethan saw his chance and dived at Kramer.

Kramer was so surprised he did nothing as Ethan slammed his fist into his jaw. Kramer fell backwards and landed heavily on the floor, dazed.

'I've been wantin' to do that since Chinn Ridge,' said Ethan, as he pounced on him. He grabbed Kramer's shirt and, rising from the floor, landed three powerful punches to the man's jaw.

But Kramer was a tough guy. As Ethan raised his fist to strike him again, Kramer bucked him off. He stumbled backwards and Kramer lashed out with his boot and tripped him so that Ethan fell back heavily on the cot. Kramer sprang from the floor and dived on top of Ethan, his hands scrabbling for his neck. As the two men's combined weight landed on the cot, it collapsed, the frame splintering into shards of wood beneath them.

The two men wrestled in the wreckage. Kramer wrapped his hands around Ethan's throat and started to throttle him. Ethan struggled, gagging as he felt his windpipe close under the pressure, but still the relentless tightening went on.

He stared up at Kramer's face, growing red with the effort of murder. Ethan grabbed his hands, tearing at his skin with his nails but Kramer did not even flinch.

Ethan felt the life in his body slowly drain out of him. The room was getting darker, his brain began to slow and for a moment he was convinced it would be easier to give up the struggle.

He took his hands away from Kramer, knowing that it was impossible to release his vice-like grip. He desperately felt around him, trying to find anything he could use as a weapon. His scrabbling hands eventually came upon a large shard of wood from the collapsed cot and, like a drowning man, his fingers grasped it. Kramer was so fixated on throttling him that he did not notice what he was doing. Summoning all his strength, Ethan brought it up like a dagger with both hands and thrust it upwards under Kramer's exposed chin.

It pierced the flesh easily. Kramer opened his mouth to scream as Ethan saw the wood go through the back of his mouth.

Kramer clutched his throat and

slowly rose to his feet. Blood was pumping over his hands, staining the front of his shirt and pants. He staggered back towards the window, hit the wall and slowly slid down, trying to speak, but the more he tried to utter sounds, the more blood flowed from his mouth.

Ethan coughed and sucked in lungfuls of sweet, fresh air. Unsteadily, he got onto his feet and crossed the room. Kramer looked up at him and reached out a hand, pleading with him to help him, but Ethan had seen enough battlefield wounds to know he was beyond help. He stared at him impassively.

'I'm sorry, Major Kramer,' he said eventually, 'this ain't politics — it's personal.'

Kramer stopped struggling as the flow of blood slowed and lay back with his eyes open. Now, it was over.

Ethan slumped to the floor in exhaustion. After a few minutes, he reached across and pulled the wooden stake out of Kramer's throat. As he did so, he heard a noise downstairs as the empty shop filled with townsfolk. There were shouts and hurried footsteps on the stairway. A group of frightened faces looked in from the doorway. Abe Skinner was the first man who dared enter the room. He stared in turn at Ethan, Kramer's lifeless body and the gun on the tripod.

'In here, fellas!' he shouted. 'I got the man who tried to kill the senator — he's murdered the major!'

23

Everything happened at once. The room was filled with people. There was shouting and pushing as men jostled to see the dead major and the man who had killed him. Ethan was too exhausted to resist as he was grabbed and hoisted to his feet. His hands were pulled roughly behind his back and tied tightly with cord.

'C'mon, boys. Let's string him up in the main street,' shouted Abe Skinner.

There was a roar of agreement and Ethan was pushed towards the door but they stopped when a small man in a frock coat stood in the doorway.

'Just what in the name of hell is going on here?' said Mayor O'Neil, looking Ethan up and down.

'He's the guy that shot at the senator,' said Abe. 'He's killed Major Kramer too. He's gonna swing for what he's done today!'

'Wait a minute, Abe. There is such a thing as the due process of the law.'

'The law? We got all the law we need. Somebody go get Sheriff Winters,' ordered Abe.

The door banged downstairs and the men heard someone running up the stairs. 'Lemme through, lemme through. Where's the mayor?'

The men made way as a young boy, red-faced and panting for breath, ran to Mayor O'Neil.

'What's up, son?' he asked.

'The sheriff, sir,' gasped the boy. 'He's dead!'

A murmur of disbelief filled the room.

'How?' asked the mayor.

'Got his head blown off. They say he was shot by a sniper.'

It seemed every eye in the room swung to look at the gun at the window and then the man they held as captive. The mayor stepped into the room and walked over to the window, stepping over the splayed legs of the major. He looked out towards the empty stage.

'You'd have to be damn good to make that shot,' he said, turning to Ethan. Ethan said nothing.

'Seems you killed two good men today, son.'

Ethan looked up. 'You didn't know them. They were double-crossing bastards who — '

Ethan's head whipped back as Abe slapped him across the jaw.

'We've heard enough, Mayor. This man's a dirty, rotten killer. He tried to kill the senator and murdered two good men. Who else was he plannin' on killin'? Looks to me as though the major came up here to stop him and this yellow-livered bastard stuck it to him.'

'That the way it was?' said Mayor O'Neil quietly.

Ethan lifted his head. 'Don't really matter what I say now, does it?'

'What you waitin' for Mayor?' cried

Abe. 'Ain't you heard enough? I say we hang 'im now!'

There was a loud roar of agreement.

'Now wait a minute! Wait a minute!' shouted O'Neil. 'Last time I looked there was something in our constitution about a man bein' innocent until proven guilty.'

'He's guilty all right! I say we hang 'im!' cried Abe.

Mayor O'Neil's protests were drowned out as men started shouting and Ethan was almost carried out of the room and down the stairs. When he stumbled to his knees he was dragged across the floor like a sack of flour and carried outside the store into the sunshine.

A larger crowd had gathered outside the street after hearing the gunshot and the hullabaloo, and when they heard there was going to be a hanging, it was as though a blood frenzy went through the mob. Someone found a rope. It was thrown up and around a rafter of a shop's false front. The noose was slung over Ethan's neck as a horse was pulled and pushed through the crowds. When it was in position, Ethan was roughly lifted up into the saddle.

Mayor O'Neil tried to shove his way to the front, shouting his protest, but he was drowned out. Abe Skinner walked to the rear of the horse and raised his hand to slap its rump. Ethan closed his eyes and prepared to be sent to oblivion. He prayed that Ruby would take care of Lucy and hoped she was nowhere near to see this. Then, he just wanted it to be over.

A gunshot rang out.

Ethan opened his eyes.

The crowd was silenced. Ethan looked at the people and realized they were all staring in the one direction. Ruby was standing on the back of a buckboard, holding a shotgun. A swirl of blue smoke was leaking out of one of the barrels.

'The man who goes near that horse again gets the next barrel in his guts.'

Abe took a few steps towards the

wagon. Ruby swung the gun in his direction.

'What in hell's name d'you think you're doing Ruby?' cried Abe.

'I'm savin' a man from doin' the Devil's jig. Cut'im down.'

'He's guilty of murder! He killed two men today!'

'Two men who should be sittin' where he's sittin' right now.'

'He tried to kill the senator, Ruby!'

Ruby shouldered the gun and pointed it at Abe. 'You got it all wrong, as usual, Abe. Your mouth is outrunnin' your sense. This man *saved* the senator's life and probably stopped this country being plunged back into a war. Kramer was part of a plot to kill the senator. Winters was in on it, too. I'll swear on the Bible.'

'But he was up in the room — with a gun — we saw it!'

Other men murmured their agreement.

'Come here, honey.'

Ruby put her hand out and pulled

Lucy up onto the buckboard beside her. 'Tell these gentlemen what happened.'

Lucy looked around the sea of faces staring at her. She glanced over at her pa. She wanted to cry but, hesitantly at first, she began to talk.

'I was kidnapped. They were gonna kill me. They told my daddy they was gonna kill me if he didn't kill the senator. I swear. It's the truth!'

A murmur passed through the crowd. People started shuffling their feet. Abe stepped forward.

'You gonna believe this? You gonna let this anarchist off with murder on the say-so of a saloon keeper and this strip of a girl? She'd say anything to save her pa's worthless neck. I say we hang 'im!'

'And I say,' shouted Ruby, 'if you hang that man today without a trial, you'll be the next to follow him to Hell!'

Mayor O'Neil stepped forward. 'People of Cotton Junction, hasn't there been enough killin' today? If we hang this man it'll be nothin' less than murder. And it won't make no difference to the men who have already died. We can give him a fair trial and, if he's guilty, then we'll do what has to be done. But you're gonna have to decide now who runs this town: the lynch mob or the law.'

There was silence. No one moved. Ruby kept the gun trained on Abe as he searched the faces around him, looking for support.

'Help me get him down,' said one of the men holding the horse.

Four men moved forward and pulled Ethan down. When his feet touched the ground, the rope was removed from his head.

'Pa!'

Lucy leapt from the buckboard and ran to her father. She ran into his chest and he pulled her tightly to him as tears started to fill his eyes.

Mayor O'Neil walked across to Abe Skinner. 'I suggest you go get yourself a drink, Abe. It's been quite a day. When

I need a jury, I'll know where to find you.'

Reluctantly, Abe gathered a few men and headed towards the saloon. The crowd began to drift away. O'Neil watched him go, then turned to the buckboard and offered his hand to Ruby.

'You are some gal, Ruby. Damnedest thing I ever saw . . .'

'Thanks, Mayor. Wasn't sure how that was going to pan out for a second or two.'

'Hope you got witnesses for the trial.'

'Plenty. Gonna speak to a certain senator. Nesbitt, over at the telegraph office, tells me there was a Pinkerton man on the train, too. They'll testify about the plot. What happens now?'

'Well, I should lock him up. Keep him in custody until the trial. But somehow I don't think he's goin' anywhere so I could let him go if somebody stands bail for him,' he said, looking at Ruby.

Ruby looked doubtful. 'Don't know

how much I could scrape together at short notice. How much you need?'

'Oh, let's see,' said O'Neil, scratching his chin. 'A dollar?'

'A dollar?' exclaimed Ruby.

'That too much?' smiled O'Neil.

'I think I can stretch to that,' said Ruby.

'Of course, if I release him, it'll have to be in your care. You'd be responsible and make sure he doesn't jump bail. You'd have to keep him close. Think you can do that?'

'I think I can, Mayor.'

Ruby walked across to Ethan, who was still hugging Lucy. He looked up when he saw her.

'You OK?' said Ruby.

'Thanks for everything you did.'

'I'm sorry I didn't believe you at the start. I just — '

Ethan shook his head. 'It don't matter.'

'Can we go home, now, Pa?' said Lucy.

'I don't know.'

'It seems I'm responsible for you now. I posted bail on condition I keep an eye on you.'

Ethan smiled. 'You gonna lock me up?'

'I don't think I'll have to do that.'

'So can we go home?'

'You can go.'

Ethan stared down at Lucy and hugged her tight, then said the words he thought he would never be able to say again.

'OK, darlin'. Let's go home.'

Clutching each other they started to walk towards the livery stable where Ethan had left the horse and buckboard in what now seemed a lifetime ago. Suddenly they stopped and turned.

'What you gonna do, Ruby?' asked Ethan.

She shrugged her shoulders. 'I ain't exactly sure.'

Ethan looked down at Lucy. 'Think we should invite Ruby home for some supper with us? Seems it's the least we can do after all she's done for us.'

Lucy's eyes lit up. 'Can we, Pa? Ruby, will ya come home with us?'

Ruby smiled, a little embarrassed, and then beamed.

'That sounds nice.'

Lucy ran towards her. 'Well, c'mon then.'

She grabbed her hand and pulled her until they were alongside Ethan. She linked her arms between Ethan and Ruby, and the three of them walked towards the livery stable together.

THE END

We do hope that you have enjoyed reading this large print book.

Did you know that all of our titles are available for purchase?

We publish a wide range of high quality large print books including:
Romances, Mysteries, Classics
General Fiction
Non Fiction and Westerns

Special interest titles available in large print are:
The Little Oxford Dictionary
Music Book, Song Book
Hymn Book, Service Book

Also available from us courtesy of Oxford University Press:
Young Readers' Dictionary
(large print edition)
Young Readers' Thesaurus
(large print edition)

For further information or a free brochure, please contact us at:
Ulverscroft Large Print Books Ltd.,
The Green, Bradgate Road, Anstey,
Leicester, LE7 7FU, England.
Tel: (00 44) **0116 236 4325**
Fax: (00 44) **0116 234 0205**

Other titles in the
Linford Western Library:

CLANCY'S LAST WAR

Terrell L. Bowers

Some crimes are too heinous to go unpunished. Morgan Clancy seeks the man responsible for the deaths of many men, including his younger brother. When the trail leads him to Bluestone Creek, his search for justice becomes entwined with the plight of local farmers and a rancher. Clancy's battle escalates when his meddling uncovers cattle theft, and endangers a young woman, her sister and father. The stakes are lethal and when the final battle comes, Clancy's trail of vengeance may cost all four of them their lives . . .

THE LAND OF LOST DREAMS

Scott Connor

Unlucky gambler Sebastian Ford owes everyone money. When Denver Fetterman calls in his debt, Ford's only option is to flee, offering his services as a guide to a wagon train of settlers. However, to repay his debts he must lead them into Hangman's Gulch, where they are to be ambushed — and, to make sure he doesn't renege, Fetterman's stalwart debt collector Chuck Kelley will go with him. When Sebastian sides with the settlers, however, only hot lead will get him out of trouble . . .